Hot Summer in the High Desert

Experience the excitement, dangers, and sins of teenagers in the '50's

by Larry Ourada

ISBN 978-1-62967-016-4

Library of Congress Control Number 2014905787

Dedication

This book owes its existence to the unique circumstances prevalent in our country in the early 1950's, when the wounds of the BIG WAR were mostly healed, and optimism and fresh energy within the population prevailed. It is specifically dedicated to the young people of that time who lived lives that were fast, exciting, and full of the turmoil of dealing with all the changes in themselves and in Society.

Special credit and heartfelt thanks belong to my daughter, Christine, and to my editor, Michelle Andresen, who spent hundreds of hours correcting, retyping, and criticizing this work. Without their continued support and encouragement, this book would never have been finished. I also want to thank Polly Hutchinson for reviewing the entire manuscript and providing invaluable suggestions and insights.

Table of Contents

Prologue

This is a historical novel about the coming of age of teenagers in the 1950's. The action takes place in Boise, Idaho, in the Hot Summer of 1952. This was a special time in a special place, during a relatively innocent period of our history- or really was it that innocent?

This novel was handwritten in 1957 and manually typed on an Olympia typewriter in 1958. It lay gathering dust until 2009, when it was resurrected and completed in 2014.

This book is not an autobiography or a memoir. While some of the events may actually have happened, the characters are a fictional composite of confused and searching teenagers. The characters should not be considered actual persons. It is intended to be a work of fiction and fancy to celebrate the magical and exciting time between childhood and adulthood.

In 1952, Boise had a population of 35,000. The big employers were the State and National governments. But, many large companies had already begun in Boise by 1952, such as Albertsons Supermarkets, Morrison- Knudson contractors (built Hoover Dam), Boise-Cascade, Simplot (potatoes and French fries). In other places, Les Schwab tire stores began in 1952, and Kentucky Fried Chicken opened its first store. McDonalds came a few years later.

The river runs right through the middle of town. World War II ended seven years before, and most of the wounds from it had healed. This Big War ended the economic depression and established the USA as the dominate World power. The military who returned had started families, and the Greatest Generation was busy building houses for themselves all across the country. "Victory Gardens", however, were still being grown in Boise by many families in back yards and empty lots. But, another war had already begun far away in Korea, wherever that is, and it was taking more young men away from their homes. Truman was President, soon to be replaced by Ike in 1953.

There were two high schools in Boise. One was a small Catholic school staffed by nuns, and one token parish priest, who said Mass daily and was allowed to teach one class—religion. The other was the large public school, which was at least twenty times the size of the Catholic one. There were no school buses to carry grade school and high school students. The students either walked to school, rode their bikes, or took a public transportation bus. The students were required to cover their school books with brown paper cut from paper bags, in order to help preserve them for the following year. Parents **never** drove their children to school. Most families, if they could afford it, had only one car.

It was before the time of dual incomes. The husband worked, and the wife was the housekeeper, cook, and in charge of raising the children.

Gasoline was .15 cents a gallon, and Detroit was busy building big cars with lots of Chrome, instead of tanks and jeeps. Turning signals had recently been invented, but not seat belts or delayed wipers.

You could buy a week's groceries for a typical family for less than twenty dollars. Anything made in Japan was junk. There were still "5 and 10 cent" stores, and you could actually buy most things in those stores for a nickel or a dime. At Albertsons, a double scoop ice cream cone was a nickel. If a penny was found lying on the ground, people would actually stop and pick it up. Most of the coins were silver, and pennies were real copper. Silver dollars were as common as paper ones. There were no espresso stands or pizza parlors, but there were a couple of drive-in restaurants, where cute car hops would come up to your window to take your order and serve you.

Copy machines, personal computers, cell phones, DVDs, video games, microwaves, credit cards, GPS, and the internet were years and decades in the future. There were telephone booths on every downtown corner, and it cost a dime to make a call. No one had thought to make designer jeans yet. In 1952, it was Levis, Dickies, and white T-shirts-not colored ones with sayings on them. Levis and Dickies cost between $3.00 and $4.00 a pair, and they were made in the USA.

Camels, Lucky Strikes, and Pall Malls were some of the favorite brands of cigarettes. The government gave them away free to the servicemen fighting the Big War. After the soldiers became addicted to them, they ended up having to pay 15 cents a pack-in 1952. Marijuana and other drugs were not around much yet. It was mostly cigarettes, beer, and booze. Only women wore earrings then, and if you had a tattoo, you had been in the Navy. You would never see a tattoo on ordinary people or sports figures.

Most bikes were one speed, with balloon tires. You rode them without helmets. You drank water from a faucet, a fountain, or a garden hose-not from a plastic bottle.

People exercised by working in their yards, and walking to the store or church, not by joining a health club to exercise with machines.

The popular comics were Superman, Batman, Flash Gordon, Wonder Woman, and 'Lil Abner.

The radio and movies were the source of popular entertainment, as television had not yet come to Boise. Bing Crosby, Johnnie Rae, Frankie Lane and the Big Bands were popular. Elvis was a few years away.

Hot Rod Magazine was four years old, but Playboy was a year away from its first issue. It was sweater girls and Bobby Soxers, rather than bikinis and bare boobs.

The big movies were mostly love stories and Westerns. Drive-in Theatres were common, and it was not unusual for four teenagers to go in one car and pay for only two, because the other two were hidden in the trunk.

If the parents could afford it, most boys in Boise got a Red Ryder BB gun by the time they were ten, and a .22 caliber rifle when they were fourteen. There were no credit cards in 1952, but credit could be established with mail order companies like Sears Roebuck and Montgomery Ward. Rifles could be ordered right out of their catalogues. They could be paid for with a monthly check of $5.00 or so until the bill was paid off, which usually took only five or six months for a good rifle. Rightly or wrongly, it was great sport hunting birds and small critters. Summer pastimes for pre-teens were making match shooters out of wooden clothes pins, playing mumbly peg with pocket knives, marbles, kick the can, and frying grasshoppers with magnifying glasses. Sometimes, on hot days, the entertainment could have been lying in the cool grass and looking up at the blue sky, watching the clouds go by, changing their shape along the way.

Boise had a minor league baseball team. Since money was always scarce, when the boys wanted to see a game, they would manage to sneak in by crawling over or under the fence. And, the team owner and the officials would let it happen and not pay much attention.

There were Little-League baseball teams, and if you were good enough, you would be picked to play on a team. If not, well, you had to deal with disappointment, and you found something else to do. A typical season consisted of ten to twelve games. If your team was lucky, some good businessman would sponsor your team and buy hats and tee-shirts so you would have some sort of a uniform to wear. Since parents had to work hard to make a living and keep up the house and garden, they rarely came to any of the games. The players either walked to the playfields or rode their bikes.

Girls did not play sports much, except for maybe tennis. If they showed any athletic ability, they usually became cheerleaders for the boys.

In the high hot desert summertime, six to twelve year olds-boys and girls both-would often leave their homes in the morning and play outside all day long with other kids in the neighborhood. They would play in the city parks, vacant lots, and in the foothills. No one could contact them all day, and they were OK. Their main rule was only to be home in time to wash up for supper.

The citizens of Boise were mostly descendants of white Europeans and Basques from Spain. There were few African Americans and Asians at that time, except for some Chinese left over from the gold and silver mining days. Agriculture had attracted a number of workers from Mexico, but they were mostly scattered around in the smaller towns in the rural areas.

If you went on a road trip, you could count on being entertained by Burma Shave or "Reno or Bust" signs out in the sagebrush along the highway.

The birth control pill had not yet been invented, and few people had ever heard of pornography or oral sex. The first Kinsey report on male sexual behavior had just been published, but the one on female sexual behavior was a year away. The Master's and Johnson's research into sexual behavior would not start for five years. In 1952, pedophile priests and Boy Scout leaders were unheard of. Gay marriages were unimaginable, and AIDS was decades away. In fact, being "gay" meant you were "fancy free." However, the start of the "Sexual Revolution" was getting real close to coming about anyway.

It was a time when young people fell in love, dated, got married, and raised a family. They did not just live together. But, nevertheless, illegitimate children were not that uncommon either.

The teachers in the Catholic schools were all nuns, and the Baltimore Catechism was considered more important to learn than the Bible. Anyone who went to a Catholic grade school definitely ended up knowing the difference between the various kinds of sins: Original, Venial and Mortal. Mortal, of course, was by far the worst, as it completely destroyed the soul and your relationship with God-it made you an enemy of God! If you were good at memorizing the questions and answers in the Catechism, you became a deep thinking Christian philosopher. You could explain the nature of the Trinity-even though it is a profound mystery! The Trinity is one Being, composed of three persons-the Father, Son, and Holy Ghost. The Holy "Spirit" came many years later with Vatican II and the charismatic movement.

In spite of the lack of sexual knowledge and training, most of the boys in Boise learned to masturbate well before puberty, thanks to older brothers and friends in the neighborhood. The problem for Catholic boys was that masturbation was always a serious sin. But, the good thing was that God was always there to forgive them through His Church, if they only went to confession and repented. And, because there were many sins of all kinds being committed by the faithful in Boise, the Church made it convenient to go to confession often.

IT WAS A SIMPLER TIME, BUT PERHAPS IN SOME WAYS MORE EXCITING THAN ANY TIME THAT CAME AFTER. A TIME WHEN YOUTH SEEMED TO BE ETERNAL AND ADULTHOOD FAR AWAY. THE TIME WAS RIGHT FOR A VERY HOT SUMMER IN THE HIGH DESERT.

Chapter One
The Party

Beyond the west the sun was starting to fade. Its waning rays were filtered by the haze of dusk, and there was a splendor of pink and orange blurred with purple hues. The day had been hot and dry. Now, through the city of Boise a cool breeze was flowing down from the green-tinted springtime hills and mountains still capped with snow.

Lenny Gibbons was standing in the bathroom combing his long wavy hair. His smooth shaven face was glowing with the quiet tension of youth. Lenny stretched his face close to the mirror to pinch out a blackhead on his nose. He had a handsome face, like the ones you see in advertisements on the back covers of slick magazines next to a beautiful poolside blonde. Lenny was quick to smile, quick to show sympathy and affection, and quick to wrinkle up with concern over some human enigma.

Lenny carefully placed a clump of greasy black hair so it hung down the middle of his forehead; then he combed back both sides so that they met in the back forming a crease, called a “Duck’s tail” or “Pachuko”. Just then a car honked outside. He rushed from the bathroom grabbing his faded blue denim jacket off a chair in the kitchen.

“Aren’t you gonna to finish your supper,” Lenny’s Mother complained.

“Naw, don’t have time. That’s Fred now. See ya later,” he said, going out the door.

“You be home early. You gotta go to school tomorrow,” his Mother shouted after him.

Lenny leaped the five front steps and ran across the lawn, hopping into the back seat of Fred’s 1934 Ford sedan. To his friends, Fred was known as “Mud”.

“Hi Mud, evening Basco, Creepy. And greetings to you Patrick.”

“Hi Len,” they said, “How they hanging?”

“Loosely, loosely,” Lenny said.

“Goose it Mud, and let’s shag-ass to the party,” Danny said, alias Creepy, reaching over and swatting Mud on the back of the head.

Mud revved up the engine and dug out in a clamor of exhaust smoke from dual straight-pipes, flying gravel, and a chirp of rubber.

"Mud, what do you use for fuel in this beast, wood," said Patrick, between sips of his beer. They each had an open can of beer already except for Lenny.

"Give me a beer ya stingy bastards."

"Yeah, give Len a beer."

"Here's a wild one Lenny Benny," Creepy said.

"Careful ya dumb dicks. C'mon don't spill it all over my car. My old man will smell it and gimme hell," said Mud.

"Eat me, Mud," said Creepy.

"Pee on your old man, but dammit, don't waste the beer!"

"Yeah, we only got a case," said Creepy.

"Only a case, Jees, whose going to drink it all?" Len said.

"Listen to Len, hell, I could drink it all my ownself," Patrick answered.

"Ha, ha, Len can't hold more than two beers without flipping his cookies," Mud said.

"I'll drink any of you pieces of caca under the table," Len responded.

"Sure as hell. Remember last New Years. Len got smashed on two glasses of whiskey so's he passed out, and we had to pack him home."

"Ah, chew mung."

"Light me up a cigarette, Basco," Mud said.

"When in hell you gonna buy yer own Mud, ya leech," said Angel Andarzo, otherwise known as Basco, the husky Basque who played fullback on the Holy Cross Football Team.

"How ya fixed for skivvies, Mud."

"Here you go, leech."

"Leech shit! When's the last time you turds bought me any gas?"

"Yer lucky we even ride in this junkheap."

"Yeah; the sonofabitch is liable to collapse anytime. Hear them pistons screaming for the last drop of oil. The bastard rattles your teeth out, the brakes are shot, and it smokes like the chimney of hell. And he wants us to pay him to ride in this bucket of bolts."

"Yeah, you oughta be happy we should lower ourselves to ride in this piece of shit."

"You guys got lots better," Mud said. "Gimme another beer, Creepy."

Mud tried to throw his empty can out the window, but it hit the top of the window, and fell down on the seat spilling out what was left in the bottom.

"Ya clumsy butthook, Mud."

"Check him, spilling beer all over the car. And him preaching to us to be careful."

"Watch out Mud! Yer going off the road!"

Mud hit the brakes, but it was too late. The car skidded down into the two feet deep barrow pit. They were on the Bogus Basin road, a mile from the city limits. It was a dirt road, and it was already dusty from the hot spring sun. In the winter it was wet from the rain and snow, and the traffic over it had worn deep ruts and chuckholes. It was almost dark now.

They all scrambled out of the car except Patrick, who just sat in the back seat and roared. No one was hurt, and the car was not damaged, but they were stuck.

"Ya dumb caca, Mud," said Basco, "Can't jalopy jockey worth a damn."

"Let's push the sumbitch out," Creepy said.

"Mud, you get in and try and back it up, and we'll all get around in front and push, if Pat will get the hell out and quick cackling! Pat, c'mon," Lenny said as he opened the door and reached in, pulling him out.

They all pushed and Mud spun the rear wheels, but the car would not move. Just then headlights struck them from around a bend in the road. Then, another pair of headlights followed. The two cars came skidding to a stop, swirling dust around the bunch of stuck teenagers.

"Who is it," Lenny asked.

"It's Jack Davis in his new car and some other guys from Boise High," said Creepy. "Hi, Jack. How the hell are ya? Mud ran us off the road. Going to the party?"

"What the hell do you think?" Then Jack scowled at Mud, and said, "Drunk already huh, Mud. Let's get this wreck on the road. You guys are holding up the action." Jack was the son of one of the richest and most influential families in Boise. He always had a new car to drive. But he was most famous because of his middle finger. He was always giving everybody the Duff.

A third car had now arrived on the scene. Most of the students wore low-hung Levis, highly polished cordovan shoes, or else suede desert boots, and white tee shirts with the sleeves rolled up, or with a pack of cigarettes rolled into them. Some of them also wore faded-blue denim jackets. They were all drinking beer and smoking cigarettes. After some pushing, name-calling and animated discussion, they all grabbed a fender here and a bumper there and heaved the belching old Ford back onto the road. By that time a fourth car came around the bend, and they all drove off up the grey, winding ribbon of road, leaving a long slow billowing cloud of dust in the darkening twilight. After another mile or so, they turned onto the road leading to Peaceful Cove. This is where the Boise High Junior Class Party was being held.

When they rounded the last corner and began winding down into the valley, there was a stream of cars a half-mile long with just enough distance apart to keep out of one another's dust.

Mud's car was then in the lead, and when it suddenly shook on the washboard road around a sharp bend, its headlights shone on a clearing swarming with teenagers. The cars that were just arriving parked in different places around the clearing, and each new arrival added to the excitement and turmoil.

Peaceful Cove was a narrow valley about a mile long and surrounded by brown barren foothills and sagebrush ten months out of the year. During these months of early spring, the sparse grass that grew on the hills became a light green. A few wild flowers broke the olive monotony in scattered clumps and wide patches. From a distance the hills looked like the texture of green tweed. There was a beauty in the hills, albeit a homely beauty. It was nothing like the grandeur of the towering Cascades to the far West, nor like the rugged beauty of the Sawtooths to the East. The foothills had a milder natural beauty that seemed more artificial than real – a beauty that murmured in varying subtle tones the basic facts of a struggling existence that happened when the hot dry summer took over. This beauty would wither quickly within a full cycle of the moon.

It was night now. The moon had risen and shone full, casting a blue hue over everything. The vast landscape could be seen clearly in its penetrating light. The sky was an azure carpet becoming profusely studded with diamond stars. Some of them were cut clean, with their facets shimmering evenly; others were roughly cut, and one or two facets would shoot their spear of silver-light farther out than the others. They were strewn on the smooth ocean floor of a black heaven as if they were ice-bits from the great glacial block of Creation by the methodic Hand of God. It was a typical desert night.

The clearing was now full of cars. They were all parked in a disorderly fashion with boys and girls sitting in them, and on them, or else running around between them.

One of the cars, a little chopped Ford coupe, began to spin around in a circle with dual pipes bellowing. The front wheels were cramped to the left, and dust and dirt was flying from the rear. Suddenly, the driver straightened out the wheels, and the car leaped out between an opening in the ring of cars and sped down the road. The teenagers began shouting and throwing beer cans at it as it left. Creepy threw his beer can and yelled, "Man, did you see him dig that crazy donut."

Most of the girls stayed in the cars, drinking beer, gabbing, and smoking. Others were necking with their boyfriends.

Lenny was sitting in Fred's car smoking a cigarette and drinking a beer and just observing what was going on. He was feeling a little sorry for coming. He had heard about these parties, and he knew that it would probably end up being just what he saw-a wild teenage kegger. But, he had always wanted to attend one and see for himself what really happened. Suddenly, Fred came and opened the door.

"Hi, Len, "he said.

"Hi, Mud, whatcha doing? Where's Creepy, and Basco?"

"I dunno, somewhere drunk on their asses probably. Where's the brew?"

"In the back seat. You better lay off Mud, you're getting gassed."

"Horseknockers," Mud said while stumbling his way into the back seat, "I'm just starting to feel good," he snickered. Then Mud began gagging, and he got up and put his head out the window just in time to vomit all over the side of the car and down on the running board.

"You dumb ass, Mud. Barfing all over the car. I knew you couldn't hold it. And you telling us to be careful and not spill any beer. Wait 'til the fellas hear about this."

After a minute or so Mud slunk back in the seat and fell asleep.

Soon, Creepy came to the car looking for beer. "Hi Creepy," Lenny said, "Mud just flipped his cookies out the window and passed out in the back seat."

"No caca, that's really humorous. Any more brew left?"

"Yeah, in the back seat."

"Where's the church key?"

"Here, where's Pat?"

"Last time I saw him he was climbing up a tree with his shirt off and muttering something about venereal wood teaching something about man, and good, and evil, or some damn thing. Damned if I know what he is talking about half the time with his big words." Danny Pankowski, more widely known as Creepy, then sat down and opened another beer.

There was now a big fire going in the clearing, and about twenty boys and a few girls were standing around smoking, drinking beer, and singing songs.

With their Levis at half-mast, most of the boys had greased down duck's tails or crew-cuts. The girls wore peddle pushers of varying colors, and blouses or white shirts with the tails hanging out and the sleeves rolled up. Some wore sweaters tight enough to bring out their best features.

"Hell of a good party ain't it," Danny said.

"Yeah, Creepy, hell of a swell blast," Lenny said.

Soon, Angel came running up all excited. "Quick Len, hand me another brew and follow me. C'mon Creepy, Spiderlegs is going to duke it out with some other turd."

"Hot damn," Danny said, "Let's go."

The three of them left and joined the already growing herd of boys and girls heading in the direction of the fight. Spiderlegs was a tall gangling series of long skin-covered bones loosely strung together by elastic strands and who's butt swung from side to side as he walked like a pendulum with the hiccups.

Jack Davis was apparently promoting the fight. He was telling the drunken Spiderlegs to beat up this other guy whom Jack did not like. The other fellow was sitting in a car with his girl. The crowd moved in.

"Go get him Spider," Jack prodded as Spider jerked the car door open. The dome light went on, and the fellow let go of his girl and turned around. He was surprised, then scared.

"Get out you no-good sonofabitch so I can kick the shit out of you," Spider said trying to sneer. It was the kind of sneer that one might see on someone about ready to throw up.

"What for, what did I do?"

"Get out!" yelled Jack as he pushed Spiderlegs aside and grabbed the poor bastard by the shirt and pulled him out into the open. "Now fight you dirty chicken," challenged Jack on behalf of Spiderlegs who stood there ready with fists clenched.

"I don't want to fight him. I didn't do nothin'. Lemme alone," the kid whined.

It looked as if the fellow wasn't going to fight, but Jack Davis would have things his way, and he pushed the scared kid into Spider. Spider immediately began flailing his arms and chopping his bony fists and elbows into the fellow's face and shoulders. The other fellow, who was shorter and huskier, began to slug back desperately. Spider wilted noticeably under his heavy blows, but he kept flinging jabs wildly enough to keep the other fellow from climbing all over him. The mob was cheering and yelling. Then, Spider quit swinging and tried to grab the kid's arms as if to stop the fight, but Jack stepped in and threw sand in the kid's face. The kid yelled, covered his eyes and stumbled backwards. He was left open and helpless, and Spider was going back after him when Jack pulled him away and started pounding the kid mercilessly as he stumbled around trying to clean out his eyes. Jack was connecting squarely with cruel blows to the kid's face and stomach. His fists cut into the kid's mouth and nose until he finally fell down. Then Jack kicked him in the balls before three other fellows went in to keep him away. The kid lay twisting and groaning while his crying girlfriend tried to help him.

Spider pushed her away and said bravely, "Had enough ya bastard? Then fade out. Flee. Get the hell outa here!" A few of the beaten kid's friends led him away and put him in his car.

"The dirty lousy bastards," Lenny whispered to Creepy, "to beat that poor kid up like that. What did they do that for?" Lenny was getting disgusted with the whole show.

"Search me," Danny replied, "Maybe the kid's Levis had been washed once too often or maybe Davis wants to diddle his girl."

"I feel like hocking a couple big goobers and splattin' them both in the eyes," Lenny muttered.

"Hang loose Len, if you get wise none of us would get outa here in one piece."

Spiderlegs took all of the credit for the triumph. He had carried out the order of his leader. Smiling complacently, he received his reward, as the crowd gathered around him telling him what a great fighter he was.

"You sure clobbered him, Spide."

"Way to go, Spidey."

"Good piece of work, Spider!"

Twisted delight and satisfaction oozed out of the corner of his sleazy smile at being the center of interest and the object of admiring associates.

There were two other fights between some juniors and some sophomores who were bold enough to crash the party. The sophomores were badly beaten up, had all of their beer stolen, and a couple of their car windows smashed before they were run out of the clearing. But, there were a few sophomores who were popular with the upper classmen or who were good athletes that were allowed to stay as guests under the protection of Jack Davis and his crew.

The group from Holy Cross Academy, were accepted because many of them were friends with Jack Davis and the other boys from Boise High who played football and basketball against them in grade school. Lenny, Danny, Angel, and Fred made up the first string backfield for the Holy Cross football team, and they were halfway respected by the public school students. Patrick was not an athlete. He had built up his stature by being a roistering good fellow and by his skill in driving cars. He won the ditch-em king title of the city and had already totaled two of his Father's cars. This all helped to enhance his prestige.

Toward midnight the party began to break up, and by one o'clock it had ceased almost completely. Only a few cars remained in the clearing, and these were filled with boys and girls feeling their way thru the mysterious delights of young passion. There were also a few who were too drunk to carry on in a grand fashion or drive away safely. They sat around the dying fire or dozed in their cars.

The beer in Fred's car was all consumed, and Danny was passed out. He slumped in a corner of the back seat with his straight mucky yellow hair mussed up and falling over his eyes to the tip of his thin brown nose.

Lenny dragged Patrick back to the car, since he was in no shape to walk. Pat mumbled something about the glory of Bacchus and the apostasy of party-pooping. He still had his shirt off, and Lenny carried it over his shoulder. Fred was now awake again, and they left for home. He stared straight ahead while he weaved down the road, and Angel's head of long twisting black hair, which defied all attempts at combing it back into a "Pachuko", bobbed aimlessly with every bump and curve.

"Want me to drive," Lenny asked.

"Hell no, I feel great," Fred replied thickly.

"You're drunk and couldn't tell your ass from a hole in the ground."

"Eat mung, Len."

Lenny wasn't going to argue at this hour in the morning, so he sat back and relaxed. He lit a cigarette, but it tasted sour and dry, and he threw it out the window. Patrick was still incoherently cursing party-poopers and singing gay and vulgar songs.

"Hey Mud, stop the car. My teeth are floating," Angel mumbled from his stupor. Fred pulled over to the side of the road, and they all got out except Danny and urinated.

The stars were more brilliant now than ever, as they shown benignly on the little group and listened to the music of four little yellow streams which ran down through the sand and into the barrow pit.

Fred took Lenny home first since he lived nearest the foothills. The house was somber and forbidding in the soft starlight. It was large and grey with black windows. He went around to the back door and opened the screen softly. The spring holding it shut squeaked with the irritation of old age at being disturbed at this hour. The floor in the porch and kitchen groaned painfully and emitted a creaking trail as he crossed into the bedroom. He undressed, threw his clothes on the end of the bed, and sank down on it. He laid there a minute thinking. He felt uneasy because he knew he could not approve of what had happened. Even though it was fun, he felt that parties like this were wrong. He was tired and his head ached, but he remembered to say his prayers. Getting up and kneeling mechanically, he laid his head on his folded hands. He mumbled through an Our Father and a Hail Mary, and then remained silently kneeling for a few minutes. His face expressed sadness. Slowly, he got up, slipped under the covers and was quickly asleep.

Chapter Two
Going Steady

The rays of the early morning sun sifted through the trees and dabbled the old brick four story academy with splotches of red and shadows of maroon.

Holy Cross Academy had stood since the beginning of the century as the only Catholic high school in Boise. The mortar between the bricks was dirty and cracking, and this added to the aspect of age and tradition of what it symbolized. Many of Boise's most prominent citizens had been educated in those classrooms and halls. As well as a good share of Boise's bar-maids, hustlers, and athletic has-beens who were once students there.

The building was a relic compared to the sprawling new Boise High with its large windows, light-colored brick walls, and soft green lawns. The girls at Boise High wore multicolored skirts and sweaters, and the boys wore Levis, faded-blue denims or suntan trousers and sports shirts or tee shirts. The girls at Holy Cross had to wear white blouses and blue skirts and blue cardigan sweaters, and the boys were required to wear their shirts tucked in their trousers. They were forbidden to wear Levis or jeans. There were a great variety of courses one could take at Boise High: shop, printing, automobile mechanics, art, and a whole variety of other vocational and fringe courses. At Holy Cross, the only choice you had was in languages, where you could take either Latin or Spanish, and in sciences, where the choice was between physics or chemistry.

There was one particular nun at Holy Cross who was especially popular with the students. Her name was Sister Josephine Mary. She had entered the religious life after the man she was to have married was killed in the First World War. She would always show up at the football games and cheer with the rest of the spectators. In her younger days, she had been a softball pitcher on a championship girl's team and after she became a nun, she still would play "burn out" with the boys in the springtime during the noon hour. She does not do that much anymore but, she still plays tennis and can move around the court quickly and gracefully even with her heavy black habit covering everything but her face and hands.

She liked presenting topics to her classes for discussion, and she was the only nun in the school who preferred to teach the boys instead of the girls. She taught the English and Religion Classes to the juniors and seniors.

The first hour this morning was spent diagramming sentences on the blackboard and in reading Gray's, Elegy Written in a Country Churchyard.

When the bell rang to end the class, the boys left noisily and crowded in among the girls in getting through the door. Some of them walked down the hall to the drinking fountain and the others congregated in a group. When the rest of the boys learned that Angel, Fred, Danny, Lenny, and Patrick had gone to the Boise High party, they all wanted to be clued in on what happened. This remained the subject of conversation and humor as the five adventurers told stories of the party at Peaceful Cove.

When the bell ran for the next class, the girls all went in promptly, but the boys lagged behind. When they did enter the classroom, they were laughing and pushing each other.

"All right, all right boys, settle down now. Class has begun. Stop your talking and get to your places quietly," Sister Josephine Mary said. The nuns never tolerated the boys being rowdy or late for class.

After they were seated, the nun walked behind her desk and sat down. Then she said, "Today we are going to talk about dating, and boys and girls going steady together." When she mentioned this subject some of the students squirmed a little in their seats. Lenny glanced over at Patrick who was almost asleep.

"I want to hear your thoughts first," Sister said, "Do you think that it's a good thing for boys and girls to go steady in high school?"

The class did not respond so Sister repeated, "Do you think that it's OK that boys and girls go steady in high school?"

One of the more intelligent, and likewise homely, girls raised her little hand and Sister called on her. She stood up (the students were obligated to stand up when called on in class) and said, "Well, Sister, I definitely don't think that they should."

"Why not?"

"Well, it isn't right. The boys should go out with different girls instead of the same one all the time, because, well, they should get to know all kinds of girls and not become attached to any particular one at our age," she said and sat down quickly.

"Well, that's true," Sister said, "Any more comments?"

No one had anything to say so she asked Patrick. She always called on Patrick when there was a lull in the discussion because he could usually dig up something to say. Patrick pushed himself up out of his desk.

"It depends, Sister. I suppose, from a Christian point of view, we should not go steady at all unless we are definitely considering marriage in the near future. And that seems very foolish to me because most of us do not know enough about ourselves, other people, the world, and what to expect in the future to make any kind of accurate judgment as to whom we would like to spend the rest of our lives with."

"Then you think that high school students should not go steady."

"Yes. In fact, the ideal thing to do would be to separate all women from all men for all their lives except for certain prescribed periods of time each year in order to give them an opportunity to reproduce the race."

The class snickered because they knew that this would start another argument between the nun and Patrick and anyone else who cared to join in. Sister rose from her chair and walked in front of the desks, and during this time she was answering Patrick.

She said emphatically, "Such an arrangement would surely destroy society. Marriage and the home are the most fundamental units of society and --."

"I disagree," Patrick broke in, "the individual is the most fundamental and important unit of Society and anything that takes away from his freedom helps destroy him, and marriage certainly places limitations on a person's freedom."

"Certainly it does," Sister replied, "but when two people marry they should freely agree to live with one another, and for each other, and to sacrifice themselves for the other person's happiness. They should freely agree to restrict their freedom and to live under the laws governing matrimony, and to perform all the obligations necessary to its proper carrying out, including raising their children properly."

Patrick did not answer. He was thinking this over and the class was silent now.

Sister continued, "When a person marries, that person chooses to marry and in every choice there is a sacrifice. Whenever a person chooses one thing for another-in this case marriage for the single life-he automatically must give up the alternative and he must accept the obligations involved in his choice, and give up the freedom of the option he has rejected."

Patrick wrinkled his brow and said, "How free do you think a man is when he decides to marry? I don't think that he's free at all. He is so full of cultural and social lies about the great romantic reservoirs of bliss in marriage, and so ignorant of the real obligations involved, and so afraid of what society will think if he doesn't marry a girl after a continuing relationship, and so hot-breathed and anxious for the rewards that his wife-to-be promises to give him that by the time he reaches the altar it is not in his power to choose against marrying."

Sister came back stronger than ever, "A man should never even begin taking girls out until he has already considered the consequences and sacrifices as well as the pleasures of marriage, and then he should decide whether or not he still wants to get married. He should do these things before he even keeps steady company with a girl."

Patrick broke in again saying slowly and deliberately, "A man's freedom of choice is so hindered by his own feelings, desires, and false notions of reality that Society thrusts upon him through the radio, the movies, and magazines that feed-and very attractively too-all the inclinations of his nature-except the intellectual-that a man can do nothing that he really should or want to do-unless he leaves Society altogether and hides himself in a cave to contemplate reality in its raw and true forms."

Seeing that the discussion was leading nowhere Sister said, "If a person cannot live in the world and still maintain his freedom of will and strong character then there must be something wrong with him. He would have to be mentally unbalanced-a psychopath. We are never tempted beyond our ability to say "no". God assures us of that. God will always give us the necessary grace to refrain from sin. And if a person is normal, he always has the ability to choose not to sin-no matter how much he is influenced by his environment. Of course, if we know that contact with a certain person or movie-whatever it might be-will almost invariably tempt us and lead us into sin, then we have the obligation to avoid those things, and we can avoid them by being diligent and alert and by asking God's help when such danger threatens."

"Now, I'd like to ask the class another question that is closely related to dating. What is your opinion on kissing?"

Patrick sat down. He was tired from the party last night and all this moralizing wearied him all the more.

Danny stood up and ventured his opinion on that, "Kissing is all right as long as they are short ones and don't lead into, well, uh, necking parties."

Some of the students smiled at this remark. Sister said, "But doesn't one kiss always lead to another until what you call "necking parties" inevitably follow?"

"Well, sometimes maybe. But, gee, Sister how would I know."

"No buts about it Danny, don't they?"

"From what I gather, I suppose they do."

One of the girls in class who was secretly engaged to a boy from Boise High raised her hand and said, "Well, Sister, do you think necking is a sin?"

"Yes, it definitely is. I don't think anyone could do that without committing a sin."

This brought a burst of objections from the class until the nun had to call for quiet and order. She was rather shocked to see that so many of her students had the opposite opinion. However, when asked to express their opinions, no one could give any good reasons to support their view, but they all felt it wouldn't necessarily be wrong to neck, as long as it didn't lead to "petting" and beyond.

Patrick or Lenny did not say anything because they both knew that necking is really only a prelude to intercourse. But, even so, Lenny had a more lax attitude toward necking because he enjoyed it so much. But every time a nun or priest would discuss the moral implications of such activity, it would disturb him. He wanted to do what was supposed to be right. As a Catholic, he wanted to save his soul. He didn't want to suffer in hell. The subject of sex and how he should form his conscience regarding it was always painful because of his own conduct during the last few years. Sure, he had first masturbated when he was eight years old, thanks to being taught by older boys in the neighborhood. But, he didn't know this was sinful then. And the times he had done it since had been confessed and the sin forgiven. But lately, he had experienced the warm and moist lips of girls and the closeness of their bodies in his arms. And, this was a thrill he now found frequently necessary to maintain his own emotional peace. When he did this he was always on guard for when his feelings were getting out of control and so far he could always stop and say goodnight. More often though, when he was out with his present girl, Karen, she would be the one to halt their caressing sessions.

Lenny's conscience had been nourished on the moral milk of the nuns ever since grade school. Now, one of them was coming right out and saying definitely that all necking was sinful. This was upsetting. Lenny's right leg began to quiver and spring up and down. This happened whenever he was sitting down and became distressed or began thinking hard about something.

Now that the students were stirred up, and she had listened to their opinions, Sister Josephine Mary began in her typical way to point out the reasons why necking was wrong.

"I see," she said, "that you students do not realize the significance of these acts of kissing, petting, and so on. They are not ends in themselves by which boys and girls can entertain each other when the dance is over or when the show lets out. These things should not be participated in, in a frivolous or light manner. These are <u>sacred</u> acts." She paused a moment to let the sacredness sink in and then continued, "They are sacred because they are the means toward a most sacred and inviolable act. These serve as the preliminaries for one thing and one thing only-the marital act."

This shocked most of the students and left them rigid in their seats. Lenny understood what she said, but he had never considered having intercourse with every girl he necked with because he knew it was wrong. Yet he desired and openly sought the enjoyment of these preliminaries.

Sister continued, "And since this is their purpose, the only lawful place where they can be practiced and should be practiced, is in the wedded state between husband and wife. Even if one person, say a boy or a girl, could kiss and not sin in doing so, he would be obligated not to do this because of the danger of causing the other party to sin. No one can know the mind of someone else, and each person is responsible for being an occasion of sin to another person, and he may not knowingly cause another person to sin. Therefore the only logical and safe thing is not to do it at all."

This brought more objection from the class, mostly along this line: How can a person tell whether he really likes a girl or she likes a boy enough to accept him or her as a life partner unless they at least kiss each other?

Sister answered, "I think you should be able to discover the personality, character, and interests of another person through normal social contact and activities, conversation and so on without kissing, and that should let you know whether or not you would want to marry the person."

"There is no need to place such an emphasis on the physical during a period of courtship. The main reason for going together is to arrive at a sympathetic understanding of each others character, habits, and total personality and not to provide each other with occasions of sin by flirting, necking, and what have you."

"Our society tends to obscure the difference between love and sex. Sex is primarily physical and selfish whereas love involves the higher emotions and the desire for the spiritual wellbeing of the other person. Real love is generous and outgoing. There are two main purposes for sex-to guarantee the procreation of the human race and to appropriately satisfy concupiscence, which is in all of us as a result of the Fall of Adam and Eve."

"Love is primarily a "willing" of the well-being of someone else. When Christ tells us to love all men, even our enemies, he doesn't mean that we should make out of the whole world a communal bed-he means that we should will or desire that good comes to them. Ultimately this means that we must want everyone to attain his foreordained end, which is the enjoyment of God in heaven. That is why it is so wrong to curse another man-to will his damnation. That is the opposite of love, that's hate."

Patrick was now stimulated enough to add some of his present notions. He stood up and said, "Sister, man is basically an animal, and the urge for sexual experience develops at an early age-far earlier than it is practical to marry in our Society. We normally have the ability to procreate the race by the time we are thirteen years old. This urge is so heightened and capitalized on by the communication and entertainment industries that a man cannot walk down the street without automatically undressing in his imagination most every girl he meets. Who is financially and intellectually prepared to marry when he is thirteen in our society? Are you trying to tell us that we should frustrate ourselves for seven to ten years, until we are prepared to marry? It's impossible to see a movie or read a magazine without participating in sexual activities. Do you advocate the sole satisfaction for these so-called "inclinations of our lower nature" to come from a purely vicarious participation? To me, this seems like it might be more dangerous to the personality than promiscuity would be, and I might add, less satisfying."

Sister fired back, "It has always been difficult to remain pure. In all ages and in all societies this problem has always existed. To obey the laws of God is hard. It will always be hard no matter what the circumstances, because of our weakened natures. The world, the flesh, and the devil are always preying on our souls. There is no easy way to happiness and heaven. Life is a journey full of pitfalls and temptations and yet, we must make the journey. And, we must make it according to God's law. It is imperative that we do so to have order in our own lives and order in society."

"The ten commandments were not given as chains to bind us from all pleasures and freedom. They are not laws only; they are guides and sign posts which we must all follow in order to might meet our destined end in the best way possible. They serve as warning signs to detour us away from the worst moral pitfalls into which we might otherwise easily fall into. Imagine a world where no one followed the natural moral laws. Imagine the anarchy that would result: injustice, lying, stealing, fornication, murder! No one would be safe or protected so that he might work toward his end in peace and security. Take the specific case of kissing, for example. How many of you boys would want your future wife, the Mother of your future children, to have been slobbered upon by every Tom, Dick, and Harry that ever took her out? How many of you girls would want a husband to be the father of your children who had pawed over every girl that he was ever alone with?"

Everyone was silent. The students still were not sure whether or not they wanted to accept her application of moral principles or not, but they felt that she had a point in her closing remarks.

Just then the bell rang and the students started to get up and leave. Sister said, “Wait a minute please, please keep your seats a moment. I want to assign a paper to be handed in next week on the six qualities you would like most in a husband or wife. We’ll discuss this further next week.”

When the noon hour came all the boys ate their lunches outside in cars along the curb. All five of the last night’s revelers were sitting in Fred’s Ford.

Lenny was munching on a big carrot that must have measured a foot long. He always brought an enormous lunch. It normally consisted of two sandwiches, an orange, an apple or a banana, carrots, cookies or cake, and a thermos jug of milk. Patrick, who was sitting beside him in the front seat never ate very much. He usually spent most of the hour smoking cigarettes.

The rest of them were quietly eating their lunches when Lenny’s leg started to quiver. Soon it was pounding so vigorously that the whole car was shaking.

“Hey Len, whatinhell you trying to do- shaking my car to pieces?” said Fred.

“Naw, Mud, it helps him digest that supermarket that he brings with him every day,” Angel replied.

Danny, who was sitting in the back seat next to Angel, reached over and swatted Lenny on the back of the head and said, “Knock it off Len, you’ll have us all shook up man. Like nervous.”

“Ouch, cut it out, ya bastard. You buggered up my Pachucko,” Lenny said. His leg kept right on shaking.

Patrick did not say anything. He just sat there looking straight ahead and smoking a cigarette. He never talked much when he was with the fellows, unless he was drunk and then it was difficult to shut him up.

“Can’t a guy think once in a while without you turds disturbing him,” Lenny responded.

“Think!” Fred said, “Hell Len, thinking only gets people in trouble. If everyone would quit thinkin’ the world wouldn’t be in such a mess.”

“How do you know Mud, you don’t know what thinking is all about,” Angel said and everyone laughed.

“Hey Mud, got a ciggy-butt?” Danny asked.

“Yeah, why?”

“Cause I want one ya stupid butthook.”

“Here you are, piece a mung.”

“Dija ever see this you guys,” Danny said, digging out a match from his pocket and striking it on his teeth and lighting his cigarette with it.

“Jees Creepy, where’d ya learn that?” Angel asked.

“I didn’t learn it Basco. I thought of it all by myself.”

“Hey, leme try that,” Fred said, “Gimme a match Creep.”

Danny gave Fred a match and whispered to Angel, “Watch this Basco.”

Fred took the match and ran it over his teeth, but it didn’t light. “No, no, Mud, hard. You have to do it hard and fast. Don’t be a chickencrap,” Danny taunted.

So Fred did it harder and it lit and burnt his lip. He yelled and everyone laughed and made fun of him. Soon, a whole group of other boys in the school approached and shouted greetings to the five in the car.

“Hi cats,” one of them said, “Hear you went to the Boise High party last night. How was it? Dija get drunk?”

There followed a discussion of the highlights of the party together with the natural embellishments that memory adds to such exciting events. This lasted until the bell rang for afternoon classes.

The next class was either Glee Club or study hall. Most of the students who could sing at all took Glee Club if for no other reason than to get out of study hall. The music instructor, Sister Angelina, was an old nun whose knowledge of music was extensive and whose love for it was excessive. She was very sensitive and was never satisfied with anything short of perfection. She became upset when a person or group sang off key or too loud or did not pronounce correctly the Latin words that composed many of the songs.

The students filed into the auditorium rather noisily and took their places. The girls sat up on tiers behind the boys, who stood on the floor in a semicircle. There were about twenty girls and fifteen boys.

The girls were all seated and about half of the boys were standing there when the bell rang for class to begin. The other boys had not yet arrived. Sister Angelina was irritated by this delay, as she had to have the group ready for the graduation exercises which were to take place in about two weeks, and there was much smoothing out to be done yet, especially with the boy's section.

Soon, the rest of the boys came in singing.

“I want a beer just like the beer that pickled my old man.

It was the beer and the only beer that Daddy ever had,

A good old-fashioned beer with--.”

"All right, all right, enough of this nonsense," screamed Sister, "Get to your places all of you and settle down. Enough, enough. You smart alecks. Can't you act grown up once in your life."

She was raging. One of the boys, Jerry Koomer, could not help smiling at her ranting, and he said, "But Sister, didn't we harmonize well?" She just stood there a minute staring and twitching a little as if she had been galvanized. Then, holding back her anger with an intense amount of will power, she said slowly and deliberately, "Get- to- your- place." They quickly took their places when she walked toward them with eyes afire and fists clenched.

All went well from then on until Lenny made a mistake and started to sing the wrong line in the middle of a Latin song.

"Stop! Stop!" Sister cried; before she could begin reprimanding him, both Lenny and Angel started laughing. It was not a very funny situation, but they could not help themselves from laughing at the frustrated facial gestures of the good old nun. "Get out! Get out! I never want to see you again. Get out!," and she chased them from the auditorium. They were scared and did not know quite what to do, but they left promptly without any argument.

"What do we do now?" Angel asked when they got out in the hall.

"I don't know, but I hope that she doesn't tell the principal. We would sure catch hell if she did. I don't know why she kicked us out anyway. Those other guys did a lot more than we did."

"Yeah, but she needs them because they can sing, especially Koomer."

"Yeah, that's right. Let's sneak down to the John and have a drag. We got time before the next class starts."

"Yeah, let's. I could use one."

Chapter Three
Football Legend

Lenny went to North Junior High in his freshman year and transferred to Holy Cross the following fall. He went to grade school with all of his best buddies at Saint Patrick's. But, he was the only one to break from the group who graduated from there. All of the others had gone right into Holy Cross. Lenny had gone to North Junior High mainly to play football. He was one of the best high school quarterbacks in the state, and was a very fast and elusive broken field runner, as well as a sharp passer. He easily made first-string at North Junior High, and proved himself to be the best ball-packer they had in years. North Junior High was many times the size of Holy Cross, and they had over a hundred students try out for the team every season. Holy Cross was lucky if they could suit up enough players to make two squads.

Even though Lenny did excel at North Junior High and his place on the varsity at Boise High was assured, he chose to go back in his sophomore year and rejoin his childhood friends at Holy Cross. His skill and his speed were even more conspicuous there because Holy Cross was in the B-league and played only the smaller schools in the southern part of the state.

Lenny was attracted by the spirit at Holy Cross which was lacking at the larger, more mechanical, and mass-producing public high schools. He thought of it as being a tradition passed down for years from one group of boys to the next ever since the 1930's when Holy Cross won the class B state championship. That year Boise High had won the class A championship, and there was proposed a charity game between the two schools at the end of the season. Holy Cross gladly accepted the opportunity to show Boise High and the whole city just how good they really were. Everyone expected them to be pulverized by the three strong platoons and heavier weight of the Boise team, and there was considerable opposition to even proposing such a mismatch. But, since it was for charitable purposes, and because many of the people in Boise wanted the chance to see Holy Cross get beaten, the game was finally scheduled for the second Saturday following Thanksgiving.

It was a very cold day, and the ground was frozen. But, there was fire in the hearts of the Holy Cross team. The glowing spirit of athletic combat was manifestly present in the players. From the opening kickoff, Holy Cross showed a surprising stubbornness against the overwhelming odds. They fought tough and hit hard on defense, and periodically baffled the bigger Boise eleven with a razzle-dazzle type of offense. But, they could not push across a score until the third quarter when they were already behind 13 to 0. Through sheer power and almost flawless execution of line bucks and off-tackle smashes, Boise had scored twice in the first half, and everyone thought they would turn it into a rout in the second half.

But the "spirit" of the Holy Cross players would not die. It animated them with unflagging energy and super-strength. They held Boise scoreless the whole second half and scored once in the third quarter on a long pass play.

Trailing 13 to 7 in the last minute of the game, Frankie Anchusi, who is Angel's uncle, galloped seventy yards to score on a play that had the whole Boise team confused. The story goes that everyone in the backfield handled the ball at least once, and none of the Boise players and few of the spectators, knew who finally ended up with the ball until they saw Frankie scampering down the sidelines with the ball well hidden between his right arm and his jersey. Holy Cross kicked the extra point and won 14 to 13.

The players on this glorious team and its fiery coach, Father Cavanaugh, are still legendary at Holy Cross, and the spirit of their football feats are still vibrating there. That's why Lenny Gibbons went back. He didn't feel this spiritual legendary motivating force at the large public school.

★ ★ ★

After school, Lenny waited outside for Karen. She was a senior, but they were both the same age and had been going together for almost two years. Finally, Karen came out of the building with another girl.

"Hi Karen," Lenny smiled.

"Hello, smart aleck," she said in a piqueing tone.

"Whatsamatter now? What did I do?"

"Don't act so stupid and ignorant. It isn't funny. You know what you did, and you should be ashamed."

"I didn't do nothin'. Why are you mad at me for?"

"Why do you have to act like a child and get thrown out of Glee Club? You boys certainly think you're smart. You know Sister began to cry after you left and called off practice because of you mean boys."

"Yeah, so I heard," he said still smiling.

"It isn't funny Leonard. Now you won't be able to sing at my graduation."

"I'm sorry, Karen. Please don't call me that obscene name, will ya. Anyway, we were just having a little fun. Can't we have a little fun once in a while? Besides, she didn't have any right to kick me and Basco out after what Koomer and those other guys did."

Karen did not say anything more, and the other girl looked at Lenny as if he was a bad little boy.

"Look," he said, "Let's forget the whole thing. I'm sorry I won't be able to sing at your graduation, and I'm sorry that I made Sister cry. C'mon, I'll walk you both down to The Cave and buy you a Coke."

"All right, we're going downtown to do some shopping anyway," Karen said.

"Fine, but don't be mad at me. I'll try to behave, but those nuns just don't understand us fellas, that's all."

They walked the few blocks to the city center where The Cave was located and had cokes. After that, Lenny asked Karen for a date for Saturday night, and then left them in front of a door to a department store and walked to the corner to catch a bus home.

The afternoon was warm and lovely. The numerous old trees that sprouted up in the residential districts stood in evenly spaced rows along the streets. They were wearing their freshest springtime green, and some of them were still bespangled with delicate white blossoms in bloom. Most of them were big contorted and twisted poplar trees that thrust themselves out over the sidewalks and streets and greeted each other with their affable grimaces. The heavy branches seemed weary under the weight of their own foliage, and they would almost caress each other, swayed by the breeze, high above the black pavement. Only a narrow strip of blue sky shown through them. They stood and leaned like lovers who have for years striven to embrace each other, but never having had that blissful satisfaction, they are eternally restless and try to sway and shimmer closer together with the help of the invisible wind.

Lenny was looking at these trees and the lawns and houses through the window of the bus as it bumped along. But, he did not notice them. He suddenly became acutely aware at this moment that he was becoming an adult and that, in the endless process of becoming, things were changing. He had changed. His friends and parents had changed. The whole world had changed. He was afraid of some of the changes, especially the changes within himself. It was becoming increasingly difficult for him to keep his mind pure and clean. He had come to know some sexual thrills the past few years. He craved more and more of them, but he had always been told they were sinful. He had begun to doubt many things he had believed, things that the nuns had taught him as well as things his parents had told him. He had never questioned anything before, and now as he began to doubt, everything became too complicated and confusing. Then too, he was becoming concerned about what to do for a career. He wanted to go to college and play football and fantasized about becoming an All-American; but other than that, he did not know what he wanted to do. All these things preoccupied him more and more.

He recalled his years in grade school when he did not have any problems. All he did then was play and have fun with his friends. They used to have great times together and got into all kinds of mischief, like running bicycles up the flagpole or dressing up like girls with lipstick, bandanas covering their hair wadded up in bobby-pins, their Levis rolled up, and even old bras filled with oranges. Then they would try to hitch-hike downtown. Those were great times! Those were the good old days!

He remembered how fast he could run, and how he won all the races at the school picnics. How he used to score the most touchdowns in their sandlot football games and how his teammates would praise him. Everyone else wanted to be on the side he was on, and when he was not a captain, he was always the first one chosen when they would choose up sides. He was still the football star, the hero; at least that had not changed.

There were some changes he liked though- the sweet tingle of holding hands with Karen in a dark theatre, the thrill of kissing her goodnight and the soft warmth of holding her close and smothering in her long blond hair, while caressing the whiteness of her neck. Yes, he liked some of the changes all right. Even an occasional cigarette and a glass of beer, or the songs that came, lingered awhile in the jukeboxes, and then departed leaving memories of true and wonderful love. Love that would last forever and sung with voices of tenderness and emotion. Then, there were the frantic and reckless jazz hits with the throbbing beats resounding from the saxaphones, trombones, trumpets, drums, and clarinets, all moaning, wailing, or thumping out swaying rhythms that would make your whole body alive so that you had to restrain yourself from the jerking, stamping, and pounding with the moving, vacillating, lovely deep rhythms. He would soar with the high, intense, prolonged blast of an agonized horn, or he might slumber under the caressing softness of a cool, velvet tenor sax. Yes, some of the changes seemed good all right.

The bus jerked to a stop at his corner, and he got off, still unaware of his immediate surroundings. Only two more weeks, he was thinking, of riding these damn things, and then school would be out for the summer. He was a little worried about what he was going to do this summer. He needed to get a job and make some money so he could buy a car, but good jobs were scarce for high school boys. He needed a car though! He needed a car more than anything else!

Chapter Four
Snooker and Rubaiyat

It was Saturday morning. Lenny got up at ten o'clock, ate a hurried breakfast, mowed the front lawn, and then caught the bus downtown. He got off the bus and walked the two blocks to the Evergreen pool hall. He was dressed in the traditional Levis and white tee shirt, and since it was going to be another warm Spring day, he did not wear a jacket.

For a pool hall, the Evergreen was a respectable and attractive place. The front of it was a restaurant with stools along the counter. There were a few booths along the wall opposite the soda fountain and two pinball machines near the entrance beside a large magazine rack. The place was clean and cheerful, with shining metal and polished formica. In the back, separated from the restaurant by a green wavy fiberglass partition, was a long and wide room filled with six pool and three snooker tables. The cloth on the tables were all new and green, and the cushions were firm and bouncy. The cue racks stood along both side-walls, and tally lines hung from the ceiling over the snooker tables. There were two or three games of pool in progress when Lenny walked in. It was too early yet to be very busy. He sat down on one of the chairs and watched the players and listened to their conversation. It was vibrant with young, innocent, vulgar prattle.

Soon, a couple of fellows from Boise High came in the back door which opened out into the alley. Lenny knew them and proposed a game of snooker with them. The winner would collect two-bits from each loser and the loser would also pay for the game. Lenny had only fifty cents to his name at the time.

Three hours later, Lenny ordered a hamburger with ketchup and fries and a milkshake. The waitress brought it back to him and set in on a shelf along the wall. He was still playing snooker and was winning as usual.

By now, the room was crowded. All the chairs were filled up with high school boys, and those who had graduated from high school, and were now in Boise Junior College. There was a great deal of noise with the racking and breaking of balls, the clacking of steel heel plates on the floor, and the laughing and talking. There was security and good fellowship here. This was a haven of amusement and companionship. It took the place of home for those who lacked a decent one. It was a place where the loose ends of living were brought together through the magic of lively discussion and friendly competition. It acted as a comfortable niche in which to escape from one's anxieties and problems.

Lenny had been winning all afternoon and had just finished beating Spiderlegs twice in a row. Spiderlegs was too awkward with his long skinny arms to develop any consistent accuracy. No one else would play Lenny at the moment, so he went over to the next table where Danny and Angel were playing a game with Jack Davis.

"How goes it," Lenny said.

"Not worth a dingleberry," Danny said.

"Lousy," Angel said.

Jack didn't say anything. He was studying his next shot. Chalking his cue, he took a drag from his cigarette and laid it on the edge of the table. He slipped the stick between his thumb and forefinger a couple of times, and then banked a red ball straight in. He looked over the table for a few seconds. There wasn't much left to shoot at. The red balls were all gone, and the deuce lay up against the rail. "In the corner," he said. He shot easy, and the cue ball tapped the deuce on the side. "Hug the rail ball," Jack coaxed. The ball crawled along the rail and dropped in the corner pocket. He missed the three ball, trying to rail it three times in the side. It was now Danny's shot. He stroked hard and the cue ball, and the three flew clear off the table and sailed down the tiled floor under the other tables.

"Dirty mung-eatin' chickenmongering pudlicker," Danny yelled.

"Hey, knock off the language," the sixty year old rack boy squeaked.

Everyone thought Danny's scratch was pretty humorous, except Danny, who hung up his cue and said, "Okay, rack 'em up. I quit. Here's yer money," and he threw some coins on the table.

"Wait up Creepy," said Angel, "I'm going witcha."

"See ya' round, like a donut," said Lenny.

"See ya Len," they said as they walked out the back door.

"Yeah, thanks for the game fellas," Jack called after them. "Care for a game Len? Five cents a point and loser pays."

"Sure. Rack! Hey, Rackboy!"

Jack was considered to be a shark at snooker, but Lenny was no slouch either. Lenny lost occasionally, but when he did he always learned from it, and he would come back the next day or so and play better than ever.

"Go ahead and break Jack. I'll give you a sporting chance before I run the table."

"Sure as hell, I average about three red balls a break."

He placed the cue ball carefully on the spot and banked it twice, so it came up behind the racked balls and struck them but slightly, leaving them barely broken. Lenny had nothing to shoot at. There were several guys watching the game. The break brought out some chatter from them, which could be summed up in, "Chickenmonger," and "Pretty sly Jack."

"Just for that I'll have to hook you," Lenny said, and he did by sending the cue ball glancing off a red one and rebounding to the other end of the table behind the three.

"Good chunk of work, Len."

Jack got out of it nicely, though, by railing the ball with good English to break up the red balls and scatter them all over the table, accidentally sinking two of them. They didn't count, however, because you have to call your shots in snooker.

"Pretty sloppy, Jack."

"Just like he played it that way." Then, it was Lenny's turn.

Lenny sank a red ball easily and played shape on the seven. He hit it straight but, not hard enough toward the corner pocket.

"Get legs, ball," he cried as it rolled to a stop just short of the pocket, and then he tried to blow it in. Jack was set up now and drove in a red ball and the five before he missed.

"Wipe the caca off your stick," Lenny sneered.

"Caca hell, when I hit 'm its just like they had eyes," Jack said.

Lenny lit up a cigarette before shooting again. He was a little nervous. He had won enough money to take Karen out tonight with some to spare, and he did not want to lose it now. He started to concentrate and plan his shots. By now there was a whole group of fellows sitting and standing around watching. Jack, however, played as smooth as the crease down the back of his long greasy hair and maintained a comfortable margin the whole game, until there remained only the five, six, and seven balls left. Jack had just run the two, three, and four, and was now fifteen points ahead. Lenny needed to beat him. He took a few seconds to analyze the table, and then neatly sank the five three rails in the side and then banked the six once back in the corner, which left him with an angle shot on the black seven that looked like it could end up in a possible scratch. He pondered the shot for a minute, decided to try it and took careful aim, sliding the cue stick slowly between his fingers. He stroked it too hard, and both balls shot into opposite corner pockets. He had scratched and lost the game.

"Shit!" he yelled.

"Tough beans Len," said Jack, "Rack!"

The old man came over and racked up the balls, while Lenny and Jack chalked up their cues for another game. Lenny was upset, and the confidence drained out of him. He lost the second game by thirty points. Lenny hated to lose any kind of contest. Especially, he hated to lose to Jack Davis who did not need the money because his parents were rich and gave him everything he wanted. Besides, he disliked Jack because he was such a popular guy for being such a dirty bastard.

" 'Nother game?," asked Jack.

"Naw, I gotta go."

"C'mon, you got time for another game. I hate to take your money without giving you a chance to win it back," he smiled.

"Yeah, I know. Some other time, I got a date tonight."

"Oh, yeah, who with?"

"Karen Fletcher."

"That blonde chick."

"Yeah."

“You been going with her quite awhile, ain’t you. Got inta her yet?”

“No. She wouldn’t let me even if I tried. She’s not that kind of a girl.”

“They’re all that kind of girl, Len.”

“She’s not.”

“Well, anyways, keep a cool tool Len.”

“Yeah, I will, keep a frigid utensil yourself.”

Lenny got a ride home with a fellow by the name of “Sparrow” Wilson on the back of his motorscooter. They called him “Sparrow” because that was what he looked like. He was small, had grey looking skin, dirty feathery hair, and a beak nose.

When Lenny got home, he called Karen and confirmed his date. After dinner, he showered and even shaved. He shaved twice a week on the average. Then he put on a pair of crisp freshly ironed denims and a checked sport shirt and carefully combed back his hair to form the perfect duck’s tail.

“Where’re you going tonight,” his Mother asked.

“Got a date with Karen. Probably to a show ‘er somepin’.”

“Why don’t you ever bring her over to the house? The only time that Pa and I have seen her is at church.”

“I could get around a little better and do a few things if I had a car of my own.”

“Have you got a job for the summer yet? Maybe if you make some money, we can help you get one.”

“Gee, really Mom. That’d be cool, real cool. The only thing is, jobs are hard to get in this town. No one wants to hire high school kids for summer jobs. I’m still lookin’ though. Well, I got to get going or I’ll miss my bus. So long.”

“What Mass do you want to go to tomorrow?”

“Let’s go to eleven o’clock,” he said as he was leaving.

All the way to the bus stop, he hated the thought of having to go on a date without a car. All the way to Karen’s house, he hated the bus ride. He despised the younger boys and girls in the bus that were giggling and talking loudly. They were all going to a cowboy movie, and it reminded him of “the good old days” when he would go downtown with all of the fellows on Friday night when they were in the seventh and eighth grades and raise hell in the theatre, and then wander around town trying to stir up a fight or run down the alleys knocking over garbage cans.

He arrived at Karen’s house a little early, and she was not ready, so he had to wait in the living room and try to think of something witty to say to her dull parents. They were always suspicious of anyone who dated their daughter, and eyed

Lenny especially close since he manifested such an obvious interest in her. Lenny thought they were boring and senile. He had been going with Karen for almost two years now, and her parents had almost come to accept him as not being too dangerous. And besides, he was a football hero, and Karen's parents thought that was in his favor.

Soon, Karen came skipping in, looking charming and gay, and rescued him from the meaningless chit-chat.

"Hello, Lenny. I hope I haven't kept you waiting too long. My what a nice evening it is. How do you like my new dress? I just love it." It was a light pink sleeveless arrangement with small white flowers on it, and it flared out at the bottom like a bell.

"I like it fine. It -uh- looks fine. Of course, you look wonderful in anything, Karen," Lenny said, as he glanced over and saw her Father wince behind the newspaper he had just picked up.

"Why, thank you, Lenny. Do you really mean it?"

"Yeah, but -uh- if you're all set, let's move out or we'll miss the show."

"Okay, I'm ready, let's go. 'Night Pop, 'night Mom."

"Goodnight kids; don't stay out late. We have to go to early mass, you know."

"I'll have her home by midnight. Okay?"

"All right. No later. Goodnight, and have a good time."

They walked the short distance downtown to the theatre and sat close to each other in the balcony. Lenny tried to nip at her neck and cheek a few times, but couldn't get much reaction.

After the movie was out, they stopped for a coke at The Cave where they met some of their friends and chatted for awhile. The place was full of teenagers and a few students from the Junior College. They were all milling around from booth to booth. Some of the older ones had been drinking and put on a loud show. It was like this most every Friday and Saturday night. The Evergreen and The Cave were the two meeting places in town for all the high school students. They would all gather at The Cave, confuse the waitress, and see who could cause the greatest disturbance. Tonight, was fairly mild, however. They were just loud and indecorous and not as subversive as usual.

When eleven-thirty came, Lenny walked Karen home through the mellow mysterious light of the retreating moon. When no cars were seen coming along the street, they would stop and kiss in the satin shadows.

The lingering sensation of the kiss was so sweet until it began to mingle within the runnels of Lenny's memory within the corruption of bitterness. The bitterness started in rivulets trickling from the darkened regions of the mind until it began swirling into the broad pool of full consciousness. The bitterness was what Sister Josephine Mary had said about kissing being wrong. Was he sinning? He did not think so. It was not a kiss of passion, but of tenderness and affection.

When they reached Karen's house, the porch light was on. Lenny did not like these last steps into the harsh brightness after the tender exhilaration of the darkness. They hesitated a moment before going up the steps; then Karen kissed him quickly, said goodnight and turned to go in. But Lenny held her and pulled her close to move within the glowing aura of her warm softness and kissed her gently and long. Then, he said goodnight softly.

He was a half-mile away before he realized how far he had gone and that he was humming softly in the dark moving shadows. It was a three mile walk home, and he suddenly broke into a fast run, dodging, and swerving as if trying to elude a host of tacklers. He came to a corner and leaped off the curb and jumped onto the next one. Then he lowered his head, and ran straight ahead as fast as he could for two whole blocks. Then he slowed down and trotted for another block breathing in the cool air. He did not want to go home yet. He felt good and wanted to do something. He thought for a minute and then decided to drop in and see if Patrick was home. Knowing Patrick, if he was home, he would probably be still up reading esoteric books and drinking beer. It was not too far out of the way and maybe Patrick would invite him to stay the night. Patrick lived in a group of large apartment buildings near the edge of town by the foothills.

Lenny walked the rest of the way enjoying the freshness of the cool night and listening to the rustle of the breeze being filtered by the leaves of the trees and the song of katydids high in the branches. One never heard these secrets in the busy clamor of the day, but only in the muffled silence of the night.

When he reached the apartment building, he saw a dim light in Patrick's window. He went into the hallway and bounded the stairs three at a time. He knocked softly on the door and heard a chair move and someone's footsteps approach.

"Who is it?"

"Me, Len, open up."

The door opened and there stood Patrick, clad in only his red, green, and brown striped undershorts, and a pair of grey argyle socks.

"Enter my good friend."

"Blessings upon you Pat. Say, those are pretty flashy shorts you have on. Just going to bed?"

"Bed? Hell no! The night has just begun, and there is much to do. That's the trouble with most people. They sleep a third of their lives away. No one who does that will ever conquer the world. Would you care for a beer?"

"Sure."

Patrick walked over to his desk where an open six-pack of canned beer was sitting. Four of them were empty and sitting in a neat row alongside the carton. The desk was further littered with an ashtray full of butts, books, and papers with notes scribbled on them, and an Atlantic Monthly magazine. One big anthology was opened at the beginning of the Rubaiyat of Omar Khayyam. Patrick opened up the last two beers and gave one to Lenny.

"Thanks Patrick. What in hell are you doing this time of night anyway?"

"I might ask the same question of you. Do you have a handkerchief? You might wipe that red stuff off your shining face."

“Oh-yeah-I-uh-been to the show with Karen and -uh- didn’t want to go home yet so I figured I’d drop by and see if you were around.”

“Oh, I see, and did you enjoy yourself?”

“Yeah, I had a good time, I guess. You do anything exciting?”

“I did. I have been exploring some of the world’s best exponents of wisdom and poetry. Would you like me to read you some poetry?” Patrick said as he tottered slightly in the middle of the room. His knees bowed in a little when he stood, and the light struck his face at an angle that showed a white scar on his forehead from an automobile accident last fall when he had rolled his Father’s new car.

“Okay, read me some poetry.”

Patrick picked up the big book and began to read aloud the one-hundred odd stanzas of the Rubaiyat of Omar Khayyam. Lenny did not realize it would take so long, and before Patrick was half through, he was a little sorry he had agreed to listen. And, before Patrick was finished, Lenny’s right leg was jumping up and down at a steady pace. Finally, Patrick stopped, put down the book, took a long guzzle of beer, lit a cigarette, and asked, “How did you like it?”

"I liked it fine. It was beautiful. The finest poem I have ever heard. In other words, I was thoroughly gassed. Only thing is-what's it all about?"

"What's it all about! Man, didn't you listen!" Then, Patrick went into a long involved explanation of the poem. He got up and began to walk in a wide circle while he expatiated and gesticulated with zealous profundity. After thirty or forty trips around the circle when he appeared to be through, all Lenny could say was, "Is that right? Well, I'll go for the loaf of bread, a jug of wine, and thou bit, but it sounds a little too pagan for me."

"By pagan, you mean un-Christian-like, is that right?"

"Yeah, I guess so."

"And by Christian, you mean a follower of Christ, is that right?"

"Yeah."

"Well, show me a living Christian if you can."

Lenny did not answer for a minute. He sipped his beer and fished out a cigarette from an open pack laying on the table. Just as he was going to answer, Patrick said, "You can't, because it's evident there aren't any. In fact, I'm beginning to think it's impossible for there to be any."

"Excuse me, while I roll up my cuffs. It's getting pretty deep in here."

"All right. If a person is a follower of Christ, then he must pattern his life after the life of Christ. Right?"

"I suppose."

"Okay then, Christ was a full-blown altruist. His whole life was devoted unselfishly toward others. He healed the sick, instructed the ignorant, and even raised the dead back to life. Then Christ sacrificed his life for all mankind in order that their sins might be forgiven and that they might attain eternal happiness. Everything He did, He did for others without any regard for His own benefit or gain. Christ was the most benevolent person that ever lived. He was a complete altruist."

"So? What is an altruist?"

Patrick stopped his pacing and looked straight at Lenny and said, "An altruist is one whose sole motivation for doing all that he does is the welfare and happiness of other people without any regard for his own welfare. It's a complete lack of egoism. And no human being can be an altruist. All their motives"-he began pacing in circles again-"are for their own damn self-interest. Everything they do, they do for self. All people are selfish sonsabitches, and therefore are not altruists, and therefore, can never imitate Christ, and therefore can never be real Christians. But, oh, how they can pretend, and mask their selfish motives and appear to be kind and charitable! What actors people are! What hypocrites! How they deceive each other into thinking that they are good and benign and gracious! They're all hypocrites-and Christians are the worst of all because they're the greatest frauds. They claim to follow Christ when they can never even come close to approaching His goodness. Why, anyone who stands up and calls himself a Christian, has committed the worst sin of all-the sin of pride-because to think of oneself as being more perfect than one actually is-is pride, and anyone who says he imitates Christ, clearly does not, because when he says it or even thinks it, he has committed an act of pride which is directly contrary to what Christ would advocate."

He stood there exhausted and trembling, but he would not sit down. Lenny was sitting on the davenport astonished at this startling revelation. He had known Patrick for a long time and knew he did some things occasionally that bordered on the deranged side, but this was a little too much to swallow in one sitting, and it made Lenny a little uneasy.

Lenny had a few doubts of his own about Christianity, but he would always try to dismiss them by prayer and was afraid to analyze them. He wanted to believe in Christ, the Church, and the forgiveness of sin. He always felt miserable after he had sinned grievously and was afraid of dying and going to the torments of hell. He needed to believe in confession because confession always brought him joy and peace of mind, leaving him free to do the more dangerous things that his young nature craved- to hunt, play football, and ride with his reckless driving friends. He was always afraid to do these things when he was in sin because of the possibility of getting killed. But after he had been forgiven in confession, he could live recklessly again as long as he did not commit a grievous sin while doing it. It was thrilling and fun to do dangerous things when he was not in a state of sin.

"Aren't you a Christian?" Lenny asked. "You go to church, and you've been raised a Catholic."

"True, I've been raised a Catholic, but I don't know if I'm a Christian or not. I have tried to believe and to practice what I have believed, but when I see all the hypocrites sitting next to me in the pew, and when I think about what man really is, then I begin to doubt whether it is possible for me to be a good Christian."

"Hell, Pat, a lot of people give their lives for the benefit of other people."

"I know-I know they appear to, but dammit, they always have as a part of their motives their own damn self-like the person who gives to charity in order to deduct it from his income taxes, or like the soldier who volunteers for a dangerous mission so he might become a hero and receive a medal. You can't get around it. There is no true altruism among humankind."

"Well, I don't know much about it Pat, but I'm beginning to think that those who cry and weep and moan over the selfishness and unkindness of people, well, they might be the greatest egotists of all."

"I detect some sharp-barbed aspersions in that last remark."

"Oh, I'm sorry, I wasn't referring to anyone in particular. I was just making an observation. Nothing to race your motor over."

Then, Patrick answered theatrically, "Oh, that's quite all right. My feelings have become calloused by the unkind cuts of those lesser individuals who do not understand. Though my head may get bloody from the blows of society, it will always be unbowed. Though my--."

"All right, okay, okay, Pat, I'm sorry if I hurt you. But you leave yourself so open sometimes that I can't resist a little jab now and then."

Patrick smiled a little and said," Yes, I know, I'm the man in the glass house all right, and when I start throwing stones around I should be more careful."

Just then there was a noise at the door. Someone was trying to turn the handle, but it was locked.

"Who's that?," Lenny asked.

"Probably my virtuous little sister," Patrick said as he walked to the door and opened it.

"And what are you doing out 'til this hour in the morning, if I may ask?"

Patrick's very cute and shapely little sister answered, "Suck eggs, crazy man. It's none of your business and besides, you bug me. Oh! Hello Lenny, I didn't see you were here too."

"Good evening, Sherry."

"Wait 'til Mother finds out about this. It's almost two-thirty and-."

"Shush up, little man, and please do put some clothes on. Why you're positively indecent," she said as she glided out of the living room and into the hall toward her bedroom.

Patrick stood there fuming. His eyes glared after his fifteen year old sister. "Damned recalcitrant, unruly, insolent youth of the modern generation," he growled.

Lenny laughed and said, "Be careful where you throw your stones, Patrick."

Patrick could see no humor in the way his sister had been carrying on lately. She was so attractive and well proportioned that she appeared to be older than she actually was, and she had been recently discovered by the boys. Patrick did not like it at all. The main reason was that he knew what the fellows were like who had been pursuing her. But, Sherry seemed like she could handle just about any situation that presented itself. Patrick knew this and that is not what worried him. What worried him was whether she could handle the strong adolescent emotions that grow like weeds among the flowers of innocence. Patrick knew what these fellows were after, and he knew that they were pretty skillful at getting it. They were mostly the son's of the richer families let out to sow the wild oats. He didn't want them defiling his only sister.

"Well, I'm out a little too late myself," Lenny said, "Perhaps I'd better be trotting along home. I enjoyed your reading to me and your beer. I'll see you, Pat."

"No, wait. Why don't you stay the night? I can't let you walk all that way home at this hour. Stay here and we'll call your Mother up and tell her first thing in the morning."

"Well, I really shouldn't."

"If you don't then I will be forced to go in and steal the keys to my Father's car to drive you home."

"You can't do that, you idiot. You don't even have a license anymore. You'd never get out of jail this time if they caught you driving again without a license."

"Then you'd better stay."

"Okay, in order that I won't force you to venture forth into the cruel world and put you in danger of being caught by the unmerciful and predatory police and get yourself in further trouble with the law, I'll stay. Which bed do you want me to sleep in?"

Patrick led Lenny into the bedroom, turned on the light and said, "Take your choice."

"Aren't you coming to bed?"

"After awhile. I'm going to read a little more."

"Okay. Goodnight. Oh, by the way, which mass are we going to?"

"Last one probably. I'll wake you in time. Goodnight."

Chapter Five
Great Burden of Reality

After Lenny had gone to bed, Patrick stayed up pacing the floor for a long time. Then he sat down at the cluttered desk and began reading The Decline and Fall of the Roman Empire. He was in the middle of the book, and he read for about half an hour. Then banging the book shut, he took out a cigarette. His fingers shook as he held the match. He noticed his hand shaking, and he tried to steady it. He held it out and stared at it. It would not hold still, and it made him angry to see it shake. "Why was it shaking? It never shook before." He always had control over himself and his body before-at least he thought he did-and it vexed him to see a part of it showing signs of tension without his willing it and even against his will. He swore at it, and then was silent for a moment. He began to chuckle and then to laugh. It was not a humorous laugh, nor was it the twisted laugh of a fiend; but, it seemed to be a strange laugh of sophisticated irony.

He was experiencing the full realization of the prison he was in- the prison with its walls of flesh and bars of bone and the wire fences of blood vessels and nerves, and the opaque sense-windows that distorted the realities and the truths that he hungered for with an unrelenting passion. His desire for truth had driven him at a premature age to begin the endless search along that road of insurmountable obstacles. His remarkably keen and rapid mind had tugged and strained at his body and dragged it and its concomitant sentiments and temperament over jagged obstacles so long that it was now bruised and exhausted. His emotions and his feelings could not keep pace with his mind, and the constant drag of them had begun to fatigue his understanding.

But, it was not only his immature emotional makeup that was a burden to his understanding; it was the new found vision and absorption of the facts of the world that were becoming unbearably burdensome and oppressive. The idealistic illusion, through which he had viewed the world of his experience, and the facts of his research made much, if not all, of the present reality distasteful, ugly, vicious, and corrupted. The more his eyes became aware of the kaleidoscopic and multifarious skin of reality, the more they fastened upon and perhaps exaggerated the defects, the errors, the hatred, the biases, the weaknesses, and the viciousness of it. He had become obsessed with these parts only and could no longer appreciate what beauty there was in the totality. But, he already saw more of its parts than the majority of mature men, and he was still but a boy. He was but a boy feeling himself being crushed by the Great Burden of Reality and unable to cope with it.

But, as mood would have it, nevertheless, there were times he could appreciate the beauties, the joys, the progress, and all those things that add a little rose-color in the cheeks of the broad face of Reality and of Fancy. He could appreciate them more than most of humanity because he had an energetic and refining intellect. But, there were times when he saw only the scars and the sneer, and these he detested with an unfathomable depth.

His was a kind and loving sensibility, and he hated the evils he saw because they ridiculed and tore the silk garments of his idealism. He hated the scars and he loathed the sneer so much that sometimes he was driven to curse the whole visage. But, the scars and the sneer would snap at him and lacerate him all the more and go beyond his point of tolerance. Life was a crucifixion during these periods. He felt chained by his own impotence and limitations to annihilate the scars and eradicate the sneer. He would feel a terrible sense of frustration, distress, and disgust. He damned the scars that marred his illusion, and he damned the snickering sneer that galled and festered his vision!

The more he became aware, the more his illusion was being shattered. The shattering of illusions is unbearable and tragic, but his was much more so, because he had a larger mind, a larger illusion of man and his environment. This illusion was not of his making alone, but it had been fostered and nourished by his parents and by the well-meaning but naiveté of many of the nuns who had taught him.

His mind was now in turmoil, and his body was a cold burnt out cauldron. He began to perspire heavily, and he became afraid. He did not know what he was afraid of or why he was afraid, but he felt scared as if he was in the claws of some wild animal that was tearing his flesh and crushing his chest. He struggled and broke loose and stumbled across the room, floundering for breath. His usually handsome face was twisted and distorted. He reached the door and almost broke the glass as he ran into it. He jerked it open and staggered a few steps, and ran down the steps to the first floor. He then leaned on the side of the building, panting and straining desperately for air. He felt he was smothering and that his chest had been crushed so that his lungs could no longer expand. He stood there a moment resting. He was tired, very tired of the world and of living. He was only seventeen, but he had acquired a very deep distorted and dark insight into himself and the world. He had the capacity and wit of a genius, but the temperament of a child. These two clashing together caused his interior struggles and his defiant quarrel with society.

After a few minutes in the cool clean night, he felt better, and the painful conflicts began to unravel themselves. He began walking slowly. His face was now impassive, but not peaceful. Rather it showed the tenseness of determined contemplation.

Suddenly, he felt cold and began to shiver. He looked down and saw that he was still clad only in his striped shorts and grey socks. He laughed as he ran back up the stairs and into the apartment. He put on a shirt and a pair of pants and sandals and went back out again. He walked through the streets of the village of apartment houses that were nestled next to the foothills and then climbed up a path leading to a viewpoint on top of a hill overlooking the village and the entire city. The sky was deep blue, and the moon-glow and star-shine transformed the whole hillside and city into various shades of blue and ebony.

At the viewpoint, Patrick sat down and crossed his legs. He thought perhaps it would be appropriate to gaze at his navel for awhile. Instead, he looked up and found the marvelous panorama of the shimmering diamond studded night sky. It was the teeming night sky of the desert which lay to the south and east. Patrick sat there and gazed and wondered about the desert, the stars, the sky, and the power of the Cause of All.

After awhile, Patrick walked back down the path enjoying the beginning of the struggle between the darkness of night and the beam-streaks of dawn.

When he reached the apartment, he was exhausted. He kicked off his sandals and fell onto the davenport and was quickly asleep.

At ten o'clock in the morning, his Mother found him still sleeping peacefully and snoring loudly. She was a rather portly and pleasant woman who was a nurse and worked in the large Catholic hospital in Boise. She began to cook breakfast and did not wake her son until it was almost ready. Then she went over and shook him gently until he mumbled some half-dozed incoherencies and vulgarities.

He finally pieced together, "Dammit, Mother, can't I have a little peace."

"It's time you woke up. It's after ten and breakfast is almost ready."

"Mother, waking up is the most harsh aspect of existence and certainly should not be practiced at such an ungodly hour."

"If you would go to bed at a decent time and undress when you do, you wouldn't feel so cranky."

"Okay, Mother, okay. Did you wake Lenny up?"

"Lenny. No, is he here?"

"Yes, didn't I tell you? He's in my room. I'll go pull him out."

He went in and did just that, grabbing Lenny by the feet and pulling him off the bed in a bundle of blankets and sheets.

"Rise and shine, Len boy. 'Tis a brand new day and ought not to be wasted in sleep. Think of all the wonderful experiences you've missed while you were asleep. You should be ashamed of yourself sleeping so late. Ah! The lassitude of modern youth! It's appalling."

"Okay, okay, hang loose Hamlet, I'm getting up."

Lenny crawled out of the mess of bedding while Patrick stood there chuckling.

"There I was," Lenny said, "I had just parked my new convertible out in the boondocks and was just putting my arm around Karen when you came in, ya big ugly turd."

They ate a fine breakfast of fruit juice, bacon, French toast, rolls, and coffee that Mrs. Shea had prepared. After breakfast, they rushed to the eleven o'clock Mass at the Cathedral. Mr. Shea was out of town on business so Patrick cajoled his Mother into letting him drive the car to church, even though he did not have a driver's license.

Mrs. Shea was not a Catholic and hence, did not go with them. It was hot by then, and the church was full of women and young girls in their colorful summer dresses and men in sport shirts and slacks or light summer suits.

After Mass, Patrick took Lenny home and then drove back home.

When Lenny went in the house, his Mother was angry. She asked him where he had been all night.

"I'm sorry Mom, I stayed with Patrick, and it was too late to call you. There's nothin' to worry about."

"You know I worry when you're not home when you should be. You should've called us."

"I told you it was too late to call. Anything to eat in the house?"

Chapter Six
Graduation

The last two weeks of school were filled with anxiety. Everyone could hardly wait 'til they were out for the summer, and the nuns had a hard time trying to get any work out of the students. Patrick's essay on the six most desirable qualities to look for in a wife was judged to be the best one written, and Sister Josephine Mary read it aloud to the whole class. But, it so happened that the day she read it, Patrick did not show up until the class was almost over. When he did come in, he was drunk and was sent to the principal's office. As the nuns will do on such occasions, the principal got extremely angry and threatened to expel him from school. But Patrick was very polite and gracious, even though he was in a stupor, and he expressed his regret so well and his resolution to never come to school drunk again that he was just sent home for the day. Also, the principal made him go see Monsignor O'Toole.

Monsignor O'Toole was the Pastor of the Cathedral, and he knew Patrick well. He gave Patrick a strong lecture, and Patrick agreed with everything he said regarding the proper and Christian way to lead one's youthful life. He agreed because he actually believed at the time that to be pure, sober, studious, and a good citizen was what he should be. He believed that was the best way for anyone to live, and he condemned dissoluteness, dishonesty, and lethargy. But, he also could not keep the curtain falling between the theory and the practice.

He was allowed to finish the school year providing he behaved himself. He did stay out of trouble until school was over, or at least he was not caught doing anything wrong.

The graduation exercises took place in the Cathedral. The seniors came down the center aisle in a slow, hesitating march, spaced a pew apart. The girls wore white gowns and the boys wore blue. They marched to the music of Pomp and Circumstance which was played by the huge organ. Then, they all sat in the front pews while hymns were sung by the Glee Club. Jerry Koomer sang his song admirably. Then, Monsignor O'Toole strode up the steps to the pulpit and began the graduation address.

He spoke slowly and deliberately about the excellent preparation provided to the students through the diligent work of the good nuns, about the mission that was before them in life, and about certain evils to avoid in the world outside. The young graduation senior class should set an example for all others that might come into contact with them in their daily experiences. Monsignor O'Toole also gave encouragement and congratulations. The round face of the Monsignor would lean forward, and his large body would spring up above the pulpit at sporadic intervals as if he was a valve on a slowly turning camshaft.

After Monsignor's address, the graduating seniors walked in single file through the gates of the altar rail, and up the steps and to the right side of the sanctuary where the Bishop was sitting in his high and elaborately carved chair with a gold mitre on his head. The seniors walked slowly up to the Bishop and knelt in front of him kissing his ring. Then they all rose, and the Bishop stood up and made a short speech. Following the Bishop's speech, was the benediction to the Blessed Sacrament and then the marching out, and it was all over. High school was over for the seniors. It would never be renewed, never be recaptured, and never to be experienced again except in the nebulous maze of memory. They were emerging out into the world now-out of their dependent and protective shells of childhood to face the world. Some were fearful, glad, or still totally unaware of what they were to find in the world, and some were overcome with nostalgia. Some of the girls shed tears the minute they reached the back of the church. Others were talking excitedly and laughing, and some were silent.

After the great congregation of students and parents, relatives, religious, friends, and well-wishers broke up from in front of the Cathedral, the seniors went down to the basement of the church to change out of their graduation robes. Some of them met with other students outside to plan for a big celebration party, and the rest of them left with their parents and relatives.

The ones who wanted to celebrate decided to drive up to the old gold-mining town of Idaho City, thirty miles away. Almost all of the twenty senior boys went, but only about half of the twenty-five senior girls, because the rest of them had to go home and celebrate with their families.

Lenny wanted to ride in a car with Karen, but all of the cars available were already packed with girls and boys. Patrick decided he would go home and steal his Father's car for the night and take Lenny, Karen, and whoever else that wanted to go with him. Fred drove to Patrick's apartment and got out to cross the ignition wires to get the car started. It was a new green Hudson Hornet. Lenny, Karen, Danny, and his girl got in the car with Patrick.

When they had driven the thirty miles to Idaho City, they tore up and down the streets, honking their horns, and squealing their tires. Then they had a short game of "ditchum" through the old narrow dirt roads of the half-deserted town. The stream of cars left the whole area breathing clouds of dust.

The only places open were two taverns. They managed to get four cases of beer from them, and then they all sped out of the darkened town of old frontier buildings and wooden cabins. They stopped along the highway by the Boise River in the midst of pine trees and built a big fire, drank their beer, and sang songs until past one o'clock.

Patrick's car was the last one to leave for the trip back to Boise. Danny and his girl, Janet, were in the front seat with Patrick. Lenny was cuddled up close to Karen in the rear.

Patrick was a skillful driver, but reckless as hell, always trying what was nearly impossible. Sometimes he succeeded- like the time he passed a big truck and trailer on the right side by driving partly on the soft gravel shoulder and partly out in the sagebrush of the desert at seventy miles an hour. Occasionally, however, he did not succeed. He had already wrecked two of his Father's cars and had gotten the present one struck three times in the springtime mud up in the foothills. It took a towing truck from town to get it out all three times, and each time his Father would scream and rave that he could not use the car anymore. The Juvenile Court had revoked his driver's license for the third time. This time, it was for a whole year, and he had nine months left before he could get it back again. But that meant little to Patrick.

Patrick could not bear to be the last one home. He began driving faster to catch up. The highway was full of curves all the way to Boise. The tires began squealing more and more on each one of them, while the passengers were being thrown one way and then another.

"You'd better slow down, Pat." Lenny said.

"Yes, Patrick, slow down!" cried Karen.

But Patrick's eyes gleamed behind the wheel. He was coming into a sharp curve forty miles an hour over the posted speed limit. They all saw the curve. No one spoke a word. Part way around the curve, the car began to slide on the pavement.

"Goose it, Pat, Goose it!" Danny yelled, while holding on tight to the door handle to keep from falling on him. The girls screamed, and Karen almost fainted. But, Patrick pushed the throttle to the floor. The rear wheels were howling for traction. Patrick hung on tight, even after the car had left the blacktop and was on the shoulder. His throttle foot was still on the floor when the car came out of the curve sideways, swerving from one side of the road to the other. He had made it, but the taillights of Fred's car were now directly in front of them. He went around it like a freight train does a tramp. Then, he slowed down because Karen was crying, and Janet had nearly wet her pants.

He drove slowly the rest of the way into Boise. As soon as they reached the city limits, a police car started following them. Soon, Patrick saw his red light turning in the mirror.

"Damn, he said," A bull is following us." They all looked around to see.

"Let's ditch 'im," said Danny.

"Okay?" Patrick said as he shifted into second gear.

"Yeah, sure," said Lenny. Just then the siren started.

"No, you will not. Stop the car at once," said Janet.

"Patrick Shea, you had better stop," said Karen. So, Patrick stopped in order to please the ladies. If there had been no girls in the car, Patrick would have not hesitated. He would either have ditched the police or smashed up the car trying. He could have turned quickly and raced for one of the roads leading up into the foothills where he could easily lose the police car among the curves and dust. But, he did not try it with the girls screaming in the car. He pulled over to the curb and waited.

A big policeman got out of his car, shuffling up to Patrick's window, while a second one remained in the squad car. He shuffled up to Patrick's window.

"Didn't you see my red light turning?" he said.

"No Officer."

"Let me see your driver's license."

"I don't have one, officer."

"You don't have one? Then, why are you driving a car?"

"I guess I wanted to. Why did you stop me? Was I doing anything wrong? I wasn't exceeding the speed limit, was I?"

"No. I stopped you to tell you your taillights were out. But, never mind that now. Did you ever have a driver's license?"

"Yes."

"Well, what happened to it?"

"A mean old judge took it away from me."

"Oh, he did, huh. Well isn't that too bad. Okay, get out of the car all of you and get in the squad car."

"Where are you taking us?"

"To the station. I'll drive your car."

The police sergeant at the desk looked angry when he saw them all come in. He was a short, but powerful Basque, and he knew every one of them, especially Patrick. One of his own daughters was a freshman at Holy Cross. He called the parents of each of them and told them to come and get their son or daughter, as the case may be. It was now three a.m.

The parents were all very irritated when they arrived at the station. They all came except Lenny's and Patrick's parents. Lenny's Mother told the sergeant to keep him in jail overnight because she was not going to come and get him. They were going to keep Patrick overnight anyway, to make sure that he appeared for court the next morning. Patrick was used to jails by now. He had been in four jails already, and he always claimed that Boise had the nicest, cleanest, and most comfortable jail in the state. Patrick maintained that he rather enjoyed jails because they were so quiet and peaceful, something like where Monks lived.

Lenny did not have to stay all night, however. Danny's Father was first to arrive and offered to take him home. Lenny was very glad. He did not mind staying all night in jail, but he definitely did not want to have to wait there and face the possibility of seeing Karen's Father. He barely tolerated her frequent dating with Lenny when they went to school dances and movies. Now that this happened, he would be even more intolerant.

Danny's Father was more sorry than he was angry. He was a lenient man who did not believe that young people could do anything wrong. He did not believe that there was any such thing as juvenile delinquency. He never disciplined Danny if Danny could give him any reason why he had done things that should not have been done. Danny was a wizard at manufacturing excuses for his misdemeanors, and his Father always believed him.

The next morning was Saturday, and Patrick had to face the Juvenile Court once again. The judge was a former Protestant chaplain in the army, and he tried his best to understand and help the boys who came before him. He had hope for Patrick because he did not seem like the rest of the boys who violated the law or infringed upon the well-being of society. Patrick was never insolent, nor did he appear to be a criminal, and the judge could see he had a great intelligence that was boiling restlessly. And, he wanted to do what he could to guide and encourage Patrick so that he might do his share to help rectify society instead of harass it. Nevertheless, he had to act in view of the record, and the record was not good-a total of seven citations for reckless driving, speeding, drunken driving, negligent driving, and so on, and now driving without a license. All his trouble had been either in his driving or in his drinking. He never stole, never willingly destroyed anything, and never got into fights.

Both of Patrick's parents were present at court. They were accompanied by the officer who had arrested him.

When they all came into the office of Mr. Neill, the Juvenile Judge rose from his chair to meet them. He did not smile.

"Good morning, Mr. Neill."

"Well, what happened this time?"

"I stopped the car that Patrick Shea was driving to tell him that his taillights were out," the officer said, "and discovered that he didn't have a driver's license. It was two a.m., and there were two other boys and two girls in the car. They had no legitimate reason for being out so late, and so I took them all down to the station. We let the others go when their parents came and got them."

"Mr. Shea, did you let your son have the car knowing that his driver's license had been revoked?"

"No, your honor, I did not. And I don't know how he got it without the keys. And, furthermore, he had better not try anything like that again or else---."

"Or else what?" Patrick said.

"Now listen here you--."

"Order! Order! We'll have none of that in this courtroom. Patrick, you hold your tongue," Judge Neill boomed. "How did you get the car without the keys?"

"I crossed the ignition wires."

"And then took it without permission and knowing full well the seriousness of your act."

"Yes, sir."

"Why did you do it?"

"I don't know sir. I guess I just felt like it."

"You just felt like it."

"Yes, sir."

"All right. I am getting tired of seeing you in this courtroom, Patrick. I've tried to be very patient and understanding with you, but you don't seem to appreciate it. You don't seem to learn. I've dealt with many juveniles in this courtroom, but you are the most incorrigible of them all. Well, the state reformatory is one place that is designed to keep people like you from harming society."

"Please, your honor, please not that," Mrs. Shea begged. She was almost in tears, "You can't do that to him. I'll make sure he's all right. I'll keep him out of trouble."

Mr. Shea and Patrick did not say anything. The judge looked at them one after another. Then he said, "Do you want to go to the reformatory, Patrick?"

"No, your honor."

"How will I know you will stay out of trouble if I don't send you to the reformatory?"

"I'll stay out of trouble. I will promise to stay out of trouble."

"You promised that before."

"He will your honor, I'll see to it," said Mr. Shea.

"Yes, your honor, we'll keep him out of trouble, only give him one more chance," said Mrs. Shea.

"All right. I'll give him one more chance," the judge said after some hesitation. "But as a consequence, his driver's license will be suspended for three more months. Now, I am warning you for the last time. If anything like this happens again, and if you are brought before me once more because of some violation of the law, then I will be forced to either send you to the state reformatory or else see to it that you leave the State until you reach the age of twenty-one. Do you understand that Patrick?"

"Yes, sir."

"Do you understand that Mr. and Mrs. Shea?"

"Yes, your honor."

"Not only that but I want you, Patrick, to report to me every other Saturday morning during the summer starting next Saturday. Every time you do not show up, you will be required to work one full day at the Central Fire Station sweeping floors, dusting, and polishing the fire trucks. Do you understand?"

"Yes, sir."

"I am sorry this has happened, and I am sorry that you have to be punished. But, until you learn to conduct yourself as a responsible and mature member of society, you will be punished, and each time the punishment will be greater. Also, I am sorry for you, Mr. and Mrs. Shea, that your son has caused you this embarrassment. Good day and remember what I told you."

"Thank you very much, your honor," said Mrs. Shea.

"Thank you, Mr. Neill. I will behave myself," Patrick promised.

Chapter Seven
Moonlight Swim

Patrick went to see Judge Neill only one Saturday that summer. He asked Judge Neill if he could be excused for the rest of the summer from reporting every two weeks. His Father worked for the state government in some kind of bureaucratic work, and he found Patrick a job which would keep him out of trouble and away from home all summer. It was with the highway department, working with a striper crew that goes all over the state and paints the white lines down the middle of the highways. The job required Patrick to be out of town traveling with the crew. Under the circumstances, Judge Neill gladly consented to excuse Patrick from reporting every other Saturday. It was a relief to have Patrick out of town and out of his hair.

Although Patrick would condone manual labor for everyone else as being healthy, creative, necessary, and productive, he himself had an aversion toward it. But, nevertheless, he was anxious to begin the job. It would be interesting to go to different places traveling around and seeing the various fascinating scenery abundant in the state they call "The Gem of the Mountains." Patrick left in the middle of June.

Lenny was lucky enough to get a job as a service station attendant at the new cut-rate gas station in town. It was Uncle Ernie's Big Wholesale Station. It sold gas for less, gave away suckers and comic books to the kiddies, and free chances on a numbers of prizes that were given away each month. The prizes ranged from oil changes to twenty gallons of gas. The sign in front said "Open 25 hours a day". They sold the most gas and paid the lowest wages in town. Lenny's starting pay was a dollar an hour, but he was happy just to be able to get a job. Summer jobs were scarce, and most of the other boys in town could not find work unless they went out on the farms, or fought range fires, or were lucky enough to get employment with some construction company. Construction jobs paid the most.

Lenny was put on the four to midnight shift. He had to work weekends and had only Monday off. Karen also got a job, working for the telephone company doing secretarial work. This pleased her Father who did not care for Karen to see Lenny any more after the incident that took place on graduation night. Since Lenny worked nights and weekends, Karen worked days, and Lenny was not welcome around her house, they did not see each other for a month. He called her once in awhile in the evening from the telephone booth at work, but he could not talk long. Since Lenny couldn't find a suitable time to take her out, he did not ask her for a date.

Nothing much happened for a month. Patrick was out of town. Lenny was working hard and did not have time for much else. He would sleep 'til around noon and maybe take a bus downtown to the Evergreen and play snooker or pool until it was time to go to work. Then he would walk to work or get one of the fellows from the Evergreen to take him. Angel and Danny were usually there, and Fred was there occasionally. Jack Davis and his followers were always there, along with a few college students home for the summer. Neither Angel nor Danny had jobs, but Fred worked in his Father's grocery store. Angel would go up to his uncle's ranch about every other week and help him for three of four days at a time. He would drive his uncle's pickup truck to the ranch and back, and was then able to use it in town.

Meanwhile, Karen was getting tired sitting home, so she accepted a date with Herbie Murphy, who graduated from Holy Cross two years earlier. He was home for the summer from college. Although she did not tell Lenny, he found out anyway and was very hurt. He did not call her for over a week, but finally, he could not stand not seeing her and switched shifts with one of the other attendants for Friday night. He called Karen on Thursday and asked her for a date. Since she had no other plans, she accepted.

Lenny was excited and anxious to see her. He needed to touch her hand and caress her warmth after so long. It had been a month-a whole month of emptiness.

Lenny had to work Friday morning in order to get off Friday night. He woke up without any hesitation at seven o'clock, because he knew that tonight would be wonderful. He was happy all day at work. When he got off at four o'clock, he decided to play a few games of snooker before going home to get ready for his date.

When he walked into the Evergreen, there was Herbie Murphy. Herbie knew Lenny and liked him. Nevertheless, he considered himself superior because of his age and his illustrious career at Holy Cross as a sports hero. He had been high-point man in basketball for three straight years while he was there. He was tall and moved gracefully and confidently. Even though Herbie thought Lenny was cool, he liked Karen, and he was not going to back off for anyone, especially someone younger, and therefore considered inferior to him. Besides, he was now in college and expected any young girl in high school to go out of their way for a chance to go out with him. Herbie had not been very successful in gaining Karen's affection on their first date, and he had called Karen up and asked her out again for this evening. He was completely frustrated when she told him that she already had accepted a date with Lenny.

Herbie wanted to remove Lenny from the picture, and here was his chance. He challenged Lenny to play a game of snooker. Lenny eagerly accepted because here was his chance to get even with Herbie for soiling the sanctity of his relationship with Karen.

Herbie let Lenny win the first game which was played for a penny a point. Lenny felt exalted and when Herbie offered to play the next game for a dollar, Lenny did not hesitate long before he agreed. Lenny was confident and very elated at the chance of vanquishing his foe still further.

Herbie won by only a few points. "Tough luck Len," he said, "want to play another game, double or nothing?"

"I-- better not," Lenny said, "I should get going."

"What's your hurry?"

"I have a date tonight."

"Oh! With who? Do I know her?"

"I think so, it's Karen."

"She is quite a chick. I had her out last week."

"So I heard."

"What time do you have to pick her up?"

"Eight-thirty. Why?"

“Eight-thirty. You got lots of time yet. It’s only a little after five. C’mon. I’ll give you a chance to get your money back. Double or nothing again.”

“Okay, Herb, I guess I’ll have to take the wind out of your sails.”

Lenny now was a little nervous. He had five dollars with him when he came in and now he did not have much money left to take Karen out. He did not have any more at home because he had deposited the rest of his last paycheck in a savings account that he started. Because he was worried, his shooting became erratic, and Herbie beat him again.

“Gee, that’s too bad, Len. Tell you what. I’ll give you another chance. One more game, double or nothing.”

This made Lenny mad. He hated to lose in anything. And to lose to the person who was becoming his rival was more than he could stand. He agreed to play again.

Lenny concentrated fully on the game. He did not see the other fellows watching and did not hear what they were saying. He only saw the six and seven balls left on the table. Herbie needed both of them to win, and Lenny needed only one. It was Lenny’s shot, and it was a straight in shot on the six. He took careful aim. The long tension had him shaky, and he shot too easy and missed. Herbie was now setup. He sank the six and then the seven and won the game.

"Well, well, you had me sweatin' that time Len. That's the way she goes. You owe me four dollars."

"Yeah, I know. I'll have to owe you four bits Herb. After I pay for the games, I'll only have three and half. Son of a bitch!"

"That's okay Len. You can pay me next time. Rack!"

This was a real catastrophe. Lenny had been beaten badly. He had lost all of his money. It was now six-thirty. He did not know what to do. Stunned, he sat down and muttered a few swear words. He had been a sucker, and now he had to call Karen and tell her. But, he could not. He couldn't tell Karen he had lost all his money and couldn't take her out! He couldn't ask his friends because they were not likely to have enough. He could go home and ask his parents, but he was prevented from doing that because they never had much to spare, and even if he offered to pay them back, his Father would have a fit. He thought he could get it all right, but he could not bear hearing his Father raging and lecturing him about the value of money. He did not know what to do. He needed Karen's tender kisses. It had been so long. Soon, Angel and Danny came over and sat down next to him.

"Still gonna take Karen out?" Angel asked.

"Hell, I don't know now."

"If you don't then why don'tcha come with us tonight. There's gonna be a big blast at Teddy Bear's pad," said Danny.

"No kidding Creepy. Well, I don't know. Damn, I'd like to take Karen out. I haven't seen her for a month. But, now I'm all wiped out financially."

"That's rough as a cob, Len. Rough as a cob," Danny said, and shook his head in sympathy.

"Listen, Len, if you do decide to go, call me up. Creepy is going to eat at my place, and we should get going. I got the pickup tonight."

"Okay Basco, only loan me a dime to call Karen, will ya?"

"Sure, only shake your buns. Say, why don't you come and eat with us, then I won't have to take you home."

"Okay. I'll be back in a second."

Lenny went and called Karen, telling her that he was sorry that he could not take her out. He said that unexpected relatives had arrived, and he had to stay home. Karen was sorry about it also, as she had wanted to see Lenny too. They made a date for Sunday afternoon to go swimming. Well, that wasn't so bad, Lenny thought. I'll see her Sunday anyway.

But, he had lied for an excuse, and this bothered him a little. He never liked to lie, but he need not confess small lies to the priest. Then, he recalled that he had not been to confession in quite awhile. He was beginning to feel a little dirty from the grime of little everyday failings, and it always made him feel pure and clean after a good confession. It shut up this conscience anyway. But, as soon as he got in the pickup with Angel and Danny, he forgot all about the lie and confession.

They were late in arriving at the large brick house where Angel lived, and Rosie, Angel's Mother, said, when they came noisily in the front door, "Angie, you're late again. Can't you ever come on time for dinner?"

"I'm sorry Mom, I tried get here on time. Lenny and Danny are going to eat with us."

"Fine," Rosie said, "Go in and wash your hands, all of you children. Scoot! Dinner is getting cold."

As usual, Mrs. Andarzo fed them royally. She liked Angel's friends, and she liked them to eat at her house and even stay overnight. She had lost her husband in the war, and her oldest son had died as a child by being run over by a car. She never remarried. Now, all she had left was Angel, and she loved him dearly. She lived in the big house with her Mother, and they were supported by Angel's uncle who ran the large sheep ranch that grandfather Andarzo had developed after he had come to this country from Spain.

At the turn of the century and thereafter, there was a large immigration of Basques from Spain to the rich valleys, prairies, and mountains of Nevada and Southern Idaho. They all worked hard raising sheep and cattle by the thousands. The first generation, through their sweat, perseverance, and privations had become rich and had accumulated vast areas of mountain and pasture land. Now, most of the second and third generations are wealthy and influential people. They were all very honest and hard working and had a serious, yet carefree attitude toward life.

The Basque tradition is still strong in these areas, but it is slowly weakening as the young people are mingling more freely with the society around them. They are all still Basque in many ways, but it is only the old people who still speak the Basque language and who preserve the beautiful songs and music of their race. Even in the young people, there is a tradition that shines quietly through their healthy skin. They have sober minds, and you can feel the placid wisdom of the centuries seeping through the wrinkles of the elderly. Their lives are orderly. They have their time for work and their times for making merry. The Basque weddings are lavish, their dances are colorful and spirited, and their picnics are gay and lively. To be a guest in one of their homes is a rare and thoroughly enjoyable treat. They know how to eat and drink, and their native foods are tangy and delectable.

The three boys ate all of their mashed potatoes and gravy, salad, hot-buttered homemade bread, and chorizos. Chorizos are Basque sausages- the most flavorful sausages in the whole world. For dessert, they had large pieces of chocolate cake, and then drank strong coffee mixed with hot milk out of large bowls with handles. They held almost three ordinary cups and had painted figures of Basques dancers on them.

After dinner, Lenny called his Mother and told her that he had eaten at Angel's and that he would not be home until later that night. Then, they all went into Angel's bedroom and spent a long time combing their hair back into Pachuckos, polishing their shoes, and just plain farting around. Later, they left in the pickup, all three in the front seat.

When they got to Teddy Bear's house, the party had already started. Ted Ferrel went to Boise High, but he was a good friend of Danny and Angel, and they all ran around together in the summertime. Ted's parents were not home, and the house was left to Ted and his sister, Gloria. Lenny had been infatuated with Gloria while they were both in junior high school. She was beautiful and alluring with long black hair. Lenny had more or less forgotten about her after he went to Holy Cross and started going with Karen, but the moment he saw her again that night, he began experiencing the tingling delights of the young concupiscence within him. She wore tight black capri pants and a tight black blouse with a white silver cross hanging from her neck. Perhaps it was the maidenform bra, as she appeared to have matured considerably since junior high school. It was easy for Lenny to forget about Karen in Gloria's presence.

Besides Ted and Gloria, there were three other girls and five other fellows from Boise High. The record player was blasting with jazz and calypsos. They were all sitting or sprawling on the couches, drinking beer, talking, and smoking cigarettes. The large front room where they were congregated was dark, and the floor was sunken and was made up of large slabs of polished flat stone. There were two big soft couches facing each other with a long coffee table between them in front of a huge stone fireplace. There were other large soft chairs placed around the room and in the corners.

A small fellow was already half-drunk and sitting next to a girl and trying to get her to neck with him, but she apparently found him to be disgusting, and she would not cooperate.

Lenny did not participate very actively in the party at first. He sat there and drank a couple of beers, talked a little with Gloria, and just observed what the others were doing. Occasionally his right leg would unconsciously shake up and down.

Danny brought out a half-case of beer from the kitchen and as soon as everyone had a fresh one, they had chugalugging contests to see who could drink their beer the fastest. Ted won the first one. He was famous for his tremendous capacity anyway. Danny, however, won the second contest. Then, all the fellows except the little one, who was still trying to make out with the girl next to him, sat on the stone floor and proceeded to sing some kind of a German beer drinking song. They would move their beer glasses around in rhythm with the catchy song, and the first one to break the rhythm or spill any beer had to chug it. Even Lenny and Gloria got in on this. With every movement or laugh, she was tantalizing, and after Lenny had drank three beers, he could not keep his eyes from filling up with her soft hair and lovely face with soft full lips. At first, he tried to keep his imagination in check and on a friendly basis, but now after a few beers, his desire began running along the natural course of sexual pleasure.

In Junior High, Gloria used to be embarrassed by the libidinal gazing of Lenny and the other boys, but now she was not. She accepted them and expected them. She had even perfected mannerisms, movements, and expressions which would intensify the growing desires of any boy who came under her spell. Her face and figure were naturally magnetic and just as a magnet draws pieces of iron, she captured the fancies of all the males within her vicinity. She enjoyed being desired and sought-after, as well as being caught. She had always liked Lenny, but in junior high, she would not let him or anyone else touch her. Perhaps she was afraid then. She had few fears now, and Lenny had heard she also had few inhibitions against allowing the boys that she liked a few liberties.

Suddenly, there was loud banging at the front door, and Ted jumped up to answer it. He opened the little barred window in the door to see who it was, then he opened the door, and cried, "Pat, you old bastard! Where the hell you been? Good to see you, you old sonofabitch! Come on in. Hey, you cats, Pat is here!"

Lenny jumped up when he heard Pat's name and ran to the door. Patrick came in singing praises to Bacchus and carrying a case of beer. After the excitement of the reunion had receded a little, Lenny asked, "How did you get home? I thought you were way up in the mountains somewhere painting highways. Don't tell me you got canned."

"Now Len, you know I am too competent of a fellow to get canned. If it weren't for my accuracy and skill, the crew I work with would never get those white lines straight."

"Then, how comes you're in town?" asked Angel.

"I refuse to answer another question until I have a cold beer!"

"Where the hells the opener."

"I don't know, hey, you wenches, where did you put the church key?"

"You put it in your pocket, Teddy Bear."

"The hell I-- oh, yeah, sure, here the sumbitch is."

After Patrick had a couple of swigs of beer, he said, "We stopped at some one-buggy logging town way out in the provincial dingleweeds somewhere for the weekend. I thought, what the hell, I don't go to work until Monday. So I hitch-hiked to Boise. I just got in town about an hour ago and came up here right away."

"How'd you know where we were?"

"I didn't know. But I can smell a beer party clear across town, so I naturally just tried to follow my nose. So, here I am, and glad to be here among you merry gentlemen and ladies."

Before long, a bunch of other fellows arrived, including Jack Davis, and the party began to get real lively. They soon ran out of beer and so a few fellows and three girls, left in Davis' new white convertible, and also Patrick's car (which he had stolen again) to get some more beer.

Gloria went along in Patrick's car with Danny, Ted, Angel, and Lenny. She sat on Lenny's lap in the back seat, which caused him to have an erection. This, of course, was embarrassing. Lenny knew she must have felt it, and he became anxious. He was afraid she'd notice. But, all she did was to settle down on it and not say anything.

While they were waiting in front of the store to buy beer, Lenny happened to glance over to his right, and there, three cars away, he saw Herb Murphy and Karen in Herb's car. Lenny's heart sunk, his stomach rose, and he felt weak all over. He began to sweat in the cool air. Lenny thought to himself "Herb had taken Karen out after all. After Herb had won all of my money, he had taken Karen out to spend it! The dirty bastard. How could he! And how could <u>she</u>!"

Lenny hoped that they would not see him with Gloria on his lap. He sank down in the seat a little, but he could still see them. Karen sat on her side of the car, but she seemed to be having a good time. She laughed often and was dressed very attractively.

Lenny longed to be with Karen. In some ways, she was not quite as lovely as Gloria, but there was something else about her that more than made up for it. Then he got mad and decided he would get really drunk. That would show her!

As they were driving back, Gloria leaned back against Lenny's chest, and he began thinking only of the soft lovely girl with the black hair that was tickling his face.

It was after midnight before they got back. Lenny and Gloria stayed in Patrick's car while everyone else got out of both cars and stumbled around in the darkness through the bushes and hedges on their way back in the house.

Lenny looked at Gloria and tried to say something, but he could not think of anything to say. He saw nothing nor thought of anything but her enticing beauty. He was afraid for a moment to try to kiss her because he tried once two years ago, and she slipped away from him and ran into her house calling a sweet, "Goodnight Lenny," to him as she shut the door. He did not want to experience that disappointment and frustration again. But, there she was close again, and this time she was smiling. He pulled her closer, and kissed her gently. He was shaking as she put her hand softly on the back of his neck and ran her fingers slowly through his long thick dark hair. This caused an extensive thrill that left him completely numb. Then Gloria drew him to her, and kissed him a long time, brushing her tongue over his lips. He was overwhelmed, defeated, completely at her mercy. Karen had never kissed him like this! When he was with Karen, he was always the aggressor, and she would always resist if he tried to get too passionate. But this, this was very dangerous! He started to tighten his arm around her, but she laughed and said, "Let's go in Lenny."

He could not say anything. He shifted his loose Levis around a bit while adjusting his stiff penis and just followed her in like a shaggy gentle dog at heel.

When they entered the dark living room, there was loud laughing and excitement. All of the fellows that stayed, while the others went for more beer, were running around in their white under shorts, and the little fellow who had been unable to find anyone to neck with was trying to masturbate in a dark corner with a limp little penis. He was completely drunk. Two of the girls that had remained were thoroughly disgusted, but one of them thought the whole situation was hilarious. Lenny was completely shocked. He had become accustomed to drinking, smoking, and necking escapades, but never anything quite so crude and wild as this.

Gloria also was repelled by such vulgar displays. But, everyone else thought it was very funny. Patrick seemed to accept what was happening, but Lenny thought his sophistication had gone too far.

Ted found it humorous, but, nevertheless thought this was just a little too obscene for his sister to view, and had the little fellow carried into a back bedroom where he immediately passed out. Then, he told the other guys in shorts to get some clothes on or get the hell out.

"Says who?" one of them said.

"Yeah, make us, fat boy."

"You better shag your buns outa here before you get thrown out," Ted said.

"Kiss my rosy red---."

He never quite finished his sentence. Ted smashed him in the mouth. He stumbled back over a chair and fell to the floor. Then, Jack Davis jerked him up by the hair and bashed in his nose so that it spouted blood. By this time, Angel, Danny, and five others had grabbed the rest of the immodest fellows and hustled them outside. They shoved them in Jack's convertible and drove off with the dual deep-tone exhausts roaring.

Patrick and Lenny remained with the girls. Patrick had drunk three or four beers by now and had another one in his hand.

"Well Pat, how's the working life?" Lenny asked.

"Great! Just Great! I recommend it for everyone. Nothing like it. Absolutely nothing."

"Work, you mean?"

"Yes, work. Manual labor. You get a feeling of satisfaction from it. In my case, I look back and for miles down the winding asphalt highways I see fresh, gleaming white lines down the middle of them, and I think-what an important service to humanity I've done today. Through my sweating hours in the hot sun, I have helped motorists to drive safer, in a orderly manner, and to stay on their own damn side of the road. It's a joy when you think of it. Why us white stripers are artists! We paint beautiful lines- kind of like Gloria's lines here-only we don't have such fine, soft surfaces to work on."

"Patrick, you've had too much beer already," Gloria said, without blushing.

"Have no fear Gloria. For the first three or four beers, I might desire the pleasure of a lovely lady such as you, but after three or four, then I crave not the delights of feminine affection but, the calming peace that comes from the beer."

"I see," Lenny said. But he did not see.

"How is Karen?" Patrick asked.

"How should I know. Besides, I don't much give a damn."

Patrick went into hysterics of laughter at this remark.

"Funnier n'hell isn't it," Lenny said.

Gloria looked at Lenny and smiled, trying to see if he still liked Karen. He did, but at the present time, his excitement over Gloria had replaced his longing for Karen's companionship.

After awhile, Jack Davis and the other fellows came back without the indecent ones they took with them.

"What'd you do with those guys," Lenny asked them.

"Ha, ha, ha," Danny hooted, "We took them downtown and made them get out of the car and walk."

"You took them downtown. Where?"

"On Eighth and Main, and we booted them out. They were still too drunk to know where they were."

"What about their clothes, they were almost naked."
"I know- ha ha ha ha---."

"You cruel things,"Gloria said.

"Yeah, they're liable to get thrown in jail, ha ha ha," Jack said.

It was not long before everyone got restless just sitting, drinking, and talking. They needed to do something exciting. It was almost two in the morning. Patrick, in his delirious state of drunkenness, suggested they all go swimming. Everyone thought this was a great idea. But where, at this time of the night? The river would be too cold, but the public Natatorium would be ideal. It was all locked up and had a high fence with overhanging barbed wire. But, that was no obstacle to the beer-soaked bravado of the group. After all, they had climbed fences before to sneak into football and baseball games, as well as wrestling matches.

"What do we do for suits," Danny said.

"Hell, I'll scrounge up some suits around here some place," Ted said. He found four or five pairs and threw them all out into the living room among the group of boys, and there was a mad scramble for them. One lamp was knocked over, and its shade was smashed, but no one bothered about it. Ted did not even care anymore. They still needed three pairs for the boys. The girls had already gone into a bedroom to change into swim suits. They came back out just in time to see Jack cutting the legs off above the knees of the three pairs of Levis that had been left by the sudden departure of their owners.

"There you go, kids. Now, we all have suits," Jack said after he was finished cutting.

All of the fellows then tromped, pushed, and shuffled into the back bedroom to get dressed. It was the room where the little fellow was passed out on the bed.

"Hey, there's whatshisname still cold," Lenny said.

"Yeah, I forgot all about him," Ted said.

"Let's take him with us and throw him into the pool."

"Naw, leave him here. He'll still be out when we get back."

They covered him with a blanket, and then left the house wearing only their swimsuits or cut-off Levis. They all went in Patrick's and Davis's cars. Lenny and Gloria went in Patrick's car. Gloria again sat in the back seat on Lenny's lap. She wore a black bathing suit and her skin was very tanned. She did not bother buttoning the shoulder straps of her suit and the front of it hung low enough to reveal the soft, deep curves of the upper part of her bosom. Lenny could not help seeing this, and it bothered him. It was a great temptation for him, as he watched the top of her breasts move up and down with her deep breathing. He tried to keep his thoughts pure, but it was difficult under such circumstances. Her bare legs were warm as they touched his and he wanted to rest his hand on her thigh. But, he was afraid of her and himself, but most of all afraid of his conscience and of God. He looked out the window away from her and thought about confession. He must now go to confession. It had been six months since his soul had been cleansed. He was always afraid to go and tell the priest his sins. The worse his sins, the more he was afraid. Sometimes he did not know how to describe some sins, and this caused part of his fear. He had committed lots of sins in six months. He had gotten drunk, neglected to say his daily prayers, had impure thoughts, had used the Lord's name in vain hundreds of times, and had done many other things that were not exactly sins, but which were mischievous or improper acts for him to be doing. Lenny thought, let's see, had I missed Mass on a Sunday? No. That's one thing. I had never intentionally missed Mass. I would never miss Sunday Mass, if there was any possible way of being present.

He had almost finished this examination of conscience when Gloria turned around and said coyly, "What are you thinking about Lenny?" She was smiling.

"Uh, nothing, it was nothing." She was lovely with her black hair falling over her shoulders. Lenny smiled back.

They arrived at the Natatorium, and they all got out of the two cars. It was dark and a little chilly, but it would start getting light from the dawn in the desert in another hour or so.

Danny, Lenny, and Jack were the first to try to climb over the wire-mesh fence which was about eight feet high. They could get their toes in between the wires and climb that way but, the barbed wire which hung over the outside of the fence for about a foot at the top, was difficult to get over. Lenny just made it, tearing one leg of his cut-off Levis as he jumped inside the fence. Jack made it too, but he ripped a gash in one hand doing it. Danny gave up and crawled back down.

"C'mon Creepy, don't chicken out," Lenny said.

"Sonofabitch! My hand hurts," Jack said.

Danny and Patrick thought it was funny that Jack cut his hand, and Jack began cursing them loudly for laughing.

Seeing that most of them would not make it over the fence, the gallant Patrick went back and got in his car, backed it up recklessly, and drove it up over the high curb around the fence at high speed. He blew out a tire and scraped the oil-pan on the curb, but he did get it close enough to the fence so that the rest of them could stand on it, and then climb over quite easily.

The light from the full moon shown through the cloudless night and flooded the pool area with a pale blue hue. They played around and swam for an hour or so, and were all sobered up by the time the first pink and rose multi-colors of dawn began tinting the Eastern sky. The water felt warm, but when they got out of it, the air felt damp and cold, and they began to shiver.

Patrick did a few absurd flops in the water from the high diving board, and then they played tag for awhile. They all had a good time. When they left the pool, there was still a little mist in the air but, it was almost daylight. They put the spare tire on Patrick's car, and then they all drove back to Ted's house.

Patrick had Ted, Danny, Angel, Lenny, and Gloria with him, and so he let all of them out at Ted's house except Lenny. Angel's pickup was still there, and Danny was supposed to stay overnight with Angel. Lenny kissed Gloria again before she got out of the car. It was a really good feeling. The night, which had started in disappointment, ended in being very enjoyable and pleasurable. He had drunk some beer, had some laughs, seen Patrick again, and enjoyed the enrapturing company of Gloria. But, he could not forget about Herbie winning all his money and then taking Karen out with it.

As Patrick started to drive Lenny home, he said, "Len, why don't you stay with me tonight?"

"Do you think it will be okay?"

"Sure it will be okay, why shouldn't it?"

"I don't know. Okay. By the way, how'd you get the car tonight?"

"When I got home there was no one there, so I just took the keys and left."

"Where's your Mother and Father?"

"Mother was working and who knows where Father is-probably out of town again somewhere."

"Saving your money?" Lenny asked.

"Most of it. Let's stop by your station. I have to buy a new tire before I go home."

"Okay."

They went to Uncle Ernie's Big Wholesale Station and had a new tire mounted to replace the one that had blown out. Then they went to Patrick's apartment and went to bed. It was 6:30 a.m., and they were both very tired.

At eight-thirty, Mrs. Shea came in. She saw the bedroom door open and walked in and almost fainted with surprise.

"Pat, Pat," she cried shaking him, "What are you doing home?"

"Easy Mother, dammit, take it easy," Patrick said sleepily.

"Why are you home?"

"I came to see you Mother dear, aren't you glad to see me?"

"Why yes, but how did you get home? Did you get fired?"

"No one has any faith in me-not even my own Mother. No, Mother, I didn't get fired. I hitched a ride home for the weekend."

"You what?"

"I hitchhiked home."

"You shouldn't have done that."

"What do you mean I shouldn't have done it? Sure, I should have done it. It was the reasonable thing to do. Where's my lovable Father?"

"He had to be gone over the weekend. He'll be home Sunday morning."

"Why the hell can't he ever stay home."

"Never mind. He has to go places with his job. Who's sleeping in the top bunk?"

"Lenny."

"Oh!, um, good morning Mrs. Shea," Lenny said sleepily, rolling over to see her through thinly slitted eyes.

Mrs. Shea laughed at Lenny. His hair was all messed up, and he could hardly open his eyes.

"Do you want some breakfast now," Mrs. Shea asked.

"What time is it?"

"A quarter to nine."

"No, no, Mother, let us sleep at least 'til noon."

"'Until noon! All right, I'm going to bed too. I'm awfully tired."

"Goodnight, Mother."

"Goodnight, Mrs. Shea."

"Goodnight, children."

Chapter Eight
Summer Afternoon

Since Lenny had to work Saturday and had a date with Karen on Sunday, he did not see Patrick anymore that weekend. Patrick stayed home Saturday night reading books and drinking beer. He left for work on Sunday afternoon with his Father, who decided to drive him back to his job rather than trust him hitchhiking. Besides, he wanted to make sure Patrick arrived there on time to work the next morning.

On Sunday afternoon, Lenny went to Karen's house. She did not appear very happy when she opened the door to let him in, and she did not greet him as warmly as it had been her custom in the past. She saw that he was brooding about something and guessed that he must have found out she had gone out again with Herbie Murphy.

"Where are the folks," Lenny asked as he sat down on the couch in the living room.

"They went for a drive this afternoon."

They sat there in silence for a few minutes. Lenny wanted to apologize for breaking his date with her, but he was too proud and hurt that she had gone out with Herbie again. So, he just sat there looking out the window.

"Are your relatives still at your house, Lenny?"

"Huh. Relatives? What—oh, yeah, I mean no, no, they left."

Karen giggled a little at the confusion that Lenny displayed. He had forgotten that he had told her that he had visiting relatives, and she knew that he had lied.

"What's so funny?" Lenny demanded.

"Nothing, what are you getting mad about?"

"Who's getting mad anyway?"

Just then the phone rang, and Karen went to answer it. It was one of her girlfriends, and she talked for a few minutes, came back and sat down at the other end of the couch. Lenny was slouched way down with his hands in his pockets, and he stared straight ahead.

"I understand you played pool Friday."

"So, what if I did," Lenny said boldly to cover up his uneasiness.

“Nothing. I guess it’s all right if you can find time and money for playing pool when you can’t find them to take me out.”

“Aw, Karen, I’m sorry—yeah, you got lots of time though. Lots of time to go out with other fellows. I know you went out with Herbie Friday night.”

“Yes, I went out with him. What am I supposed to do. After you called and gave me a flimsy excuse for breaking our date, Herb came over and asked me out. He said he had won all your money playing snooker and that you probably wouldn’t be able to take me anywhere. That made me mad, so I went out with him. Besides you lied, you didn’t have any relatives visit you.”

“Okay, so I lost my money, and so I lied. What was I supposed to do when I didn’t have any money? I really wanted to take you out, but I couldn’t after I’d lost all my money. I’m really sorry, Karen. I haven’t seen you for such a long time. I’ll never let that happen again.”

“I guess I will forgive you, Lenny. But, you can’t expect me to stay home all the time waiting for you, can you? If you wouldn’t have lied and just told me what had happened, it would have been all right. We could have stayed home and gone for a walk or something. I like you very much and would like to see you more often. But, I told you I wouldn’t go steady because going steady is wrong if we're not planning to get married someday."

"Yeah, I guess you're right. But it shook me up losing to Herb, and I couldn't think of what to do."

"I know, that's all right."

"I like you very much, Karen."

"Lenny, I --."

He kissed her three or four times and then held her for a few minutes, and then tried to kiss her again. She resisted saying, "No, no, Lenny, you mustn't. We shouldn't do this so much. It's not right."

"I know—but I need you so much. I've missed you so much."

"I've missed you too, but, say," she said breaking loose, "you were supposed to be taking me swimming."

"I know, what time is it?"

"After one-thirty, why?"

"I have to go to work at four. We don't have much time."

"Okay, let's play some tennis. It's not too hot today, and I have two rackets."

"Okay, let's go."

"Okay, wait 'til I put on my Bermuda's."

They walked over to a park about six blocks away and played tennis for about an hour. Then, they sat in the shade of a big poplar tree for awhile, and Lenny walked her back home. When they reached her house, she made some lemonade, which they drank before Lenny had to go to work.

While walking to work, Lenny's thoughts wandered back to what Karen had to say about their kissing. He realized that kissing and necking were definitely wrong if done indiscriminately and excessively. Sister had said it could even be sinful. What an ugly word- Sin! He could not help but think that a lot of things were good, or at least not bad, until some priest or nun would come along and call it sinful. Then he had to disapprove and try not to do them because he was trying to be a good Catholic. It seemed there was hardly anything you could do that was any fun without it being a sin. The very ring of the word echoing through his thoughts was repelling. Lenny thought whoever invented such a harsh and poisonous word, anyway? Some damn killjoy adult probably. Adults are the cause of all the troubles in the world. They make the laws, don't they? If there weren't any laws to break, everyone would be happy and could do as they pleased. Or could they? Hell, he did not know. Take for example, kissing. It was pleasurable and thrilling if done properly, and it was impossible to do without it. He never wanted to kiss a girl five years ago, but, now it was different.

He needed kisses now. When he was alone and thinking about it, his conscience would make him decide that it was wrong, and he should not do it. But when he was with Karen, and the other night with Gloria, he was compelled to engineer his thoughts in order to bottle up these dictates of his conscience, and he would go ahead and do these things and enjoy them. Later, however, the many pronged scruples would always appear to jab him and cause him mental pain. However, with each occurrence, the barbs would seem to become duller, and his conscience would seem to become more callused until, on some occasions, they did not disturb his peace of mind a great deal anymore.

Then, something would happen to tear the calluses loose or poison the barbs again. Like Karen's remarks about their kissing, or a spiritual retreat at school, or a lecture by a nun. Then, the delicate consciousness would be sick and painful until he was driven into the confessional. He must go to confession soon. It had been a long time. The burden of small sins was becoming oppressive and stifling. He said three Hail Mary's, while he sauntered lazily along watching the squirrels running across the lawns and up and down the trees. The fat, gnarled, and twisted locust trees were reaching, ever reaching further up toward the yellow sun and the fresh blue sky.

Just before reaching the gas station, the word "marriage" flashed into his mind. It flickered there in big bright red neon lights. He stopped and stared ahead at nothing. Karen mentioned something about marriage. He never thought seriously of it before. This would be the means of satisfying the growing desires of his virile body and eliminate at the same time, the main source of his temptations and consequent spiritual torments. This would be the solution, the way out. But, this frightened him. He was only seventeen! He ran the rest of the way to work, as he used to run home through the dark streets at night when he was a child. He became frightened of the silence, and the unknown that lurked behind every twisted tree or preyed in the denseness of the gloomy undulating branches, or stirred within the mute mobility of the wind.

Chapter Nine
The Hot Rod

Lenny worked at the station until the end of July. During this time, he did not do much else. He saw Karen about once a week and still went to the Evergreen occasionally. He would sleep ‘til noon almost every day. Sometimes, though, Angel or one of the other boys who went to Holy Cross would come to his house and get him out of bed at nine o’clock in the morning to go golfing. Boise had only one public golf course, but it was a large one with long fairways and cool rippling creeks running through it, and ponds to drive over with frogs and big sluggish carp in them. It was refreshing to be out there in the morning when you were fanned by a gentle breeze, before the sun reached its height and crushed out the sparkle of the dew and warmed the sweet morning breath from the mountains.

Lenny would have worked longer at the gas station had he not been fired. He had washed Uncle Ernie’s big black Lincoln one day, and when he backed it out of the garage, he scraped its rear fender and the side of it on an oil can rack that had been left in the way. It took off some of the paint, leaving a crease in the metal. The Manager reported this to Ernie.

"Tell that careless kid he will have to pay for it to be repaired," yelled Ernie.

When told this by the Manager, Lenny responded, "Why should I have to pay for it, since it wasn't my fault. Someone left the oil can rack sitting in the doorway of the garage."

The Manager retorted, "That doesn't matter. Ernie said you will have to pay to get it fixed or you won't be working here anymore."

Lenny replied, "Ok, that's fine with me. Make out my check, and I'll be on my way."

Lenny was getting tired of the job anyway and was almost happy to be fired. He did regret, however, losing the chance to make some more money to save for college. He knew that he would not find another job for the month before school started again. Lenny was hopeful of getting an athletic scholarship to the University of Idaho, anyway. So, he didn't worry too much about having the money for college. Lenny really did want to go to college. If he had another good year in football, he was sure that he would be offered a scholarship. Lenny already had some feelers from some of the Basque alumni who had played football at the university. They had seen him in some of his games and had come into the locker room to pat him on the back and congratulate him for a good game.

When he told his parents he had been fired, his Mother became angry at the Manager and Ernie because they wanted Lenny to pay for repairing the damage on the car. His Father got mad at Lenny for denting the fender in the first place, and then quitting in the second place. Then, his Mother became angry at his Father for getting mad at Lenny. A tremendous argument ensued, with the result being that his Father was mad at everyone and his Mother mad at everyone but Lenny. Lenny was mad at no one and found the whole situation hilarious.

The next day, Lenny brought home a 1932 Ford coupe with no fenders or running boards, and with a chopped top and dual exhaust. The windshield was only seven inches high, and the only paint on it was old faded red undercoat. The tires were bald, and it burned a quart of oil every hundred miles. But, it had a Ford truck V-8 engine, mated to Lincoln Zephyr gears in the transmission. It was very fast out of the gate and would lay rubber in every gear. The Ford belonged to one of the young men from the junior college, and Lenny wanted to buy it. It was a real cool machine.

When he showed it to his parents, they both laughed at it. But, their laughter ceased when Lenny told them that he wanted to buy it. They told him they would not have a contraption like that on the premises and to quit being silly.

Lenny said, "I'm not being silly Mother. I like it. I think it's a really neat hot rod, and I'm going to buy it."

"It looks like it's more shot than hot," his Mother responded.

"What you want anything like that for," his Father said, "Why, it hasn't got no fenders, and listen to the noise it makes. You'd kill somebody in a contraption like that. It's a hunk of junk, and I don't want to have anything to do with it. What the hell is it anyway?"

"It's a 1932 Ford."

"A 1932 Ford! What kind of engine, a Model B?"

"No, a 1948 truck V-8."

"A V-8! They're no damn good. I never did like V-8's. The pistons wear the cylinders lopsided, and they're too hard to work on."

"Hell, Pa, they've been putting V-8's in all the new cars for years. They wouldn't do that if they weren't any good."

"Sure! You know why? 'Cause they wear out faster and cost more to fix up. So the mechanics can make more money, that's why. Huh, I know these new cars. There ain't none of them any damn good. Why don't you find a Model "A" to buy?"

"There's no use arguing Pa. I'm going to buy it. I can buy it for only seventy-five dollars."

"What! Seventy-five dollars! You can get cars like that at any junk yard for ten- and with fenders too."

"Yeah, but they ain't chopped and hopped up like this one, Pa. I want it, I got the money, and I'm going to buy it."

"Damn kids nowadays anyway. Think they can do anything they want. When I was a boy -- ."

"Now shut up, Pa," his Mother broke in, "and quit yer cussin'. Let him buy it if he wants it. It's his money, and besides, it is kinda cute."

"Kinda cute, hell! I'll never ride to church in that thing," his Father said as he went storming in the house, slamming the screen door.

So Lenny bought the car. The first thing that he did was to go and pick up Angel, Danny, and Fred, and show them the car. Danny got in the front seat, while Angel and Fred sat in the turtleback in the rear. Lenny roared through town once, leaving a black cloud of smoke at each stop light, and then headed for the foothills.

“Len, this goes like a bomb, what’s it got in it?”

“Dual dipsticks, high speed bumper bolts, full-race fanbelt, and high-compression radiator cap.”

“No crap! No wonder it takes off like a herd of turtles.”

“Yea, it goes like a bat outa hell.”

“Where ya going,” yelled Fred from the turtleback.

“Hill climbing,” Lenny yelled back.

“Hot kersnatch!”

“Snot kerhatch!”

The foothills were dry and brown now. They had lost the ephemeral beauty of spring, and the green grass had been burnt brown by the hot desert sun. There were many roads through these foothills that were steep, rough, and dusty. There was no apparent reason for the existence of all these roads, but they did serve at least two purposes. They were a good test for the power and ruggedness of automobiles, and they supplied convenient havens for young lovers during the quiet seclusion of the summer nights.

Lenny took his chopped “deuce” up over the toughest roads around. It bounced, spun, and roared over every steep grade it came to until the water in the radiator started to boil, and they had to stop. When they scrambled out and opened the hood, they saw that there was a leak in the radiator. There was not any water anywhere near them. The nearest creek was a mile away over about five hills, and the road they were on did not go to the creek.

They stood around swearing and laughing at their predicament for a few minutes, and then Fred decided he had to urinate. He walked to the rear of the car and was unbuttoning his pants, when he turned around and yelled," Hell, I'll help fill up the radiator with piss."

They all thought that this was a wonderful idea from such a dumb bastard, and they laughed hilariously while Fred climbed up on the front wheel, straddled himself over the hood, and unloaded his burden. Since Fred was laughing too, he failed to aim all of his contents into the hole, and part of the urine ran down the side of the hood and down the front of the grill. Then, they all followed him in turn and urinated in the radiator the best they could. This did not go very far in filling it up, however. Then, Lenny remembered he had brought a six pack of beer along. It was all hot, shaken up, and not fit to drink. So they opened up the beer, and squirted each other with it until it quit fizzing, and poured the rest of it in the radiator. Then they started back toward the city to tell everyone about Len's new hot rod.

★ ★ ★

That Friday night, Lenny took Karen out to a drive-in movie in his "new" car. At first, she did not like the strange looking thing and almost refused to even ride in it. It hurt Lenny to have her disapprove of his finest possession. He thought that it was the coolest car in town and was very proud of it. When he would go down the street, everyone would turn around and look at it. Other cars going in the same direction would pull way over and let it pass, and those coming from the opposite direction would move over next to the curb on their side of the street. Wherever he would park it, there would always be young boys congregating around it and looking it over and asking Lenny to "Rap it up" when he left. Lenny felt like he was really somebody now that he had his own hot rod.

Karen did not understand Lenny's enthusiasm and pride over such a queer looking thing. But, nevertheless, they went to the drive-in movie, and enjoyed it and each other.

Lenny was so elated over his new car and the freedom and prestige he thought it brought him that he forgot all about going to confession on Saturday. He spent the whole day painting his car with the spray attachment from his Mother's vacuum cleaner. He thought he had bought flat red undercoat, but it turned out to be a bright glossy orange. When he finished painting it, he thought it looked beautiful.

After dinner, even though it wasn't completely dry, he drove it downtown to the Evergreen. He was so delighted and confident over his car that he won every game of snooker he played. He even beat Herbie Murphy two games, and this made him even more elated. He was in his moment of glory, like the times he would burst through the line, swerve, dodge and kick his way past the secondary. Then, dash the rest of the way for a long touchdown run, hearing the wild yells from the crowd. He felt above the world and its problems, above the people around him, and above the traffic on the street.

Chapter Ten
Basque Picnic

Sunday was warm. The sky was cloudless and painted in cool deep shades of blue. A velvet-smooth breeze caressed the city and swirled among the trees, filtering through them, and dispersing itself among the houses to meet again along the broad quiet streets and avenues. It would then try to climb the foothills to the north, only to be checked in the net of high dry grass and thrown back through the city again in mild confusion to wander among the people and the things of people once more. Then through its indefatigable formlessness, the breeze would find the freedom and flatness of the desert to glide and cavort and chase the lazy tumbleweeds and wander blindly over the plains and through the valleys, drinking from the fluid coils and swirls of the mighty Snake River. Then on and on, until the breeze would lose itself forever to struggle and die in the wilds and mountains of Utah and Wyoming.

★ ★ ★

It was the day of the annual Basque picnic to be held in the green and shade of the city park. The Basque people began arriving around noon. The tables were set up, and the beer and ice cream trucks arrived and began to dispense their wares to the grownups and children. The old Basque grandmothers began gathering around a big table, talking excitedly in their native tongues, while the old Basque men would find a table of their own and do the same. Others were getting out the food and plates. They started drinking beer, telling stories and renewing old acquaintances. Some of them had not seen each other for a long time, as many of them lived on ranches up in the mountains or worked on construction in other parts of the state. They would all gather together in this fashion twice a year, at the annual summer picnic and at the Sheepherder's ball, which occurred in December. About the only other times they ever all got together would be at some big wedding or funeral.

People kept arriving all day long. Most of them were Basque, half-Basques, or non-Basque, who were friends of the Basques. The Monsignor and three other priests also came. One of them was a Basque priest who had recently come over from Spain to help out with the growing Basque congregation. He did not speak much English yet and went around to everyone greeting them in the colorful Basque language. His lack of English wasn't that important, since a big part of his pastoral duties involved traveling around the state, hearing confessions, saying Mass, and giving sermons in the Basque language.

Someone offered this priest some wine in a botie, a pear shaped flask of animal hide, and the priest took it and put it up to his mouth, letting the narrow red stream of wine flow into it. He then gradually lifted the container farther from his mouth, until he held it up at arm's length with the stream of wine flowing about two feet into his mouth. Then, he lowered it slowly until it touched his lips again, stopping the flow, without spilling a single drop. The crowd clapped and shouted congratulations in Basque. The priest smiled and offered the botie to Monsignor O'Toole to try it.

Monsignor O'Toole shook his head saying, "No, no, I will not be able to do that," and everyone laughed all the more.

Soon the games began, and it was at this time that Lenny, Angel, Danny, and Fred, arrived in Lenny's orange hot-rod. They went over to where Angel's Mother, grandmother, uncles, aunts, and all their many diversified offspring were, and helped themselves to some sandwiches and beer that were offered them. Then, they wandered around from place to place talking to the people they knew and helping themselves to more beer and food. Everyone was happy, gay, and carefree.

First, there were races for the young boys: foot-races, three-legged races, and sack races. Then, the adults took over and had horse shoe throwing contests, egg and water balloon throwing contests, and races.

Following these came the main event- the traditional tests of strength that are so popular among the Basque people. Basque men are strong and muscular, and they pride themselves in their strength. When the boys are approaching manhood, their muscles begin to bulge and harden and their chests expand until they are like thick steel barrels.

Angel was no exception to this. His body had lost its plump softness in the last two years, and his muscles were no longer supple and flowing with movement, but were hard and quick with power. He was like a marble statue of some Greek athlete who had left its pedestal to compete and live again. Among any other group of people, he would have been conspicuous for his physique, but when in a crowd of his own race, he was only one among many.

One of the tests was to lift a solid iron ball, almost the size of a bowling ball, from the ground, with one hand, up over the head. This took skill, balance, and strength. The hardest part was to get it off the ground and as high as the shoulder without it rolling off one's hand. If you once got it that high, it was easy to grunt, jerk, and raise it above your head.

The men took turns trying to lift it, while the people would crowd around in a big circle and cheer or taunt in either English or Basque. Only three men succeeded in raising it with only one hand. One of them was a professional wrestler, one was Gus, the short but heavily built police sergeant, and the other was a giant among the Basque sheepherders who stood around six feet seven inches high. He stood, a handsome bachelor, over the whole crowd, and he always had a group of young women near him the whole afternoon. Lenny and Angel tried it when the men were through, but neither of them could lift it above their waists. Some young Basque girls stood watching them and admiring them. They laughed and giggled when Lenny and Angel could not lift it.

Late in the afternoon, after everyone had eaten and were relaxing, the old grandmothers and grandfathers, with plump bodies and wrinkled faces, gathered around three big wooden tables and sang old Basque Ballads. Some of them sounded sad, others were gay, told of love, of labor, or of the death of a loved one. They were sung with such feeling they seemed to transport one out of the park, out of Boise, and across the ocean to another land.

Toward evening, the excitement and tempo of the picnic began to pick up momentum. A big wooden platform was set up on the lawn, and a Basque band began setting up its instruments getting ready for the dancing which was to begin soon. The priests had left a long time ago, and many of the children had gone home with their grandparents. The young and middle-aged men and women remained, because for them, the fun was just beginning. Some sheepherders were still arriving from the hills in their Levis and colorful plaid shirts. Some of them still wore their working boots.

Lights were turned on around the dancing platform and around the beer and chorizo booths. The music began to clang, tinkle, and boom in an almost furious rhythm. La Hota! La Hota! The people began yelling, and the floor soon became crowded with people.

It was at this time that Ted Ferrel and Jack Davis came driving into the park with a couple other fellows. Gloria and two other girls who were at the party at Ted's house were with them. They parked their car and joined the group of people gathered around the dance platform and the beer booth. They all bought cans of beer and were standing around before Angel spotted them.

Angel, Danny, and Fred ran over and greeted them.

"How the hell are ya, cats?"

"How they hanging?"

"Swinging side by side. What you been doing?"

"Good evening, ladies."

"Looks like a lively party."

"A real ball."

"You look like you're really livin' it up, Mud."

"He's already drunk."

"What d'ya mean, drunk," Mud said as he tried to give Angel a shove, missed, and almost fell to the ground bumping into a husky Basque and causing him to spill part of his beer.

"Hey, slow it down, young fella," the Basque said.

"I'm sorry, I-- I didn't mean to," Mud said still trying to stand up straight.

"See Mud, you're so smashed, you can't even stand up," Ted said and the rest of them laughed and pushed him around a bit.

"Where's Len?"

"Lenny Benny? The last we seen, he was doing the La Hota."

"Yeah, he's had so much beer, he doesn't know what he's doing anyway."

"No crap. This I have to see," Ted said.

They all pushed their way through the crowd that stood around the platform.

"Where is he?"

"There he is, ha-ha-ha-," said Danny convulsing with laughter.

Lenny was kicking his legs, going around in a circle, and snapping his fingers, which got the young girl partner almost as confused as he was. Everyone was laughing at him because he didn't know what he was doing. But, he was feeling good and having a great time. His partner was a black-haired dark-eyed little Basque Beauty, and she was laughing at him too. She would catch Lenny when they circled and came together as the rhythm of the dance changed and carry him into the right step, and when they parted again turning this way and that, snapping their fingers and shifting their feet in a furious pattern of motion. She would laugh at him trying to copy the swift and complex movement. She danced the La Hota briskly in her colorful Basque costume of a bright red full skirt, billowy sleeved soft white blouse, with a black leather waistcoat laced up the front, and black ballerina slippers laced to mid-calf.

When the music stopped, the crowd was still laughing at him, but Lenny was smiling, and didn't mind being laughed at. He was having fun! Angel yelled at him, and Lenny looked over and waved. Then he walked the girl back to her place, thanked her very much for dancing with him, pulled up his sagging Levis, tucked in his shirt, and started back across the platform where Angel, Danny, and the rest of them were standing.

Before he got across, the music started again, and he was in the middle of the frantic and gay dancing. He made his way across the floor staggering and dodging the dancers as best as he could.

When he got down off the platform and greeted the group, he was puffing and his thick hair was disheveled and falling over his forehead and ears.

"Hey, Len, you really looked good out there," Angel said.

"You really think so, Basco. Why the hell don't you try it? It's great sport."

"You won't get me out there. That's rougher than any football game."

"Why, you're panting, Lenny. What's the matter?" asked Gloria smiling.

"I'm not in shape for that kind of thing, I guess," Lenny said, looking into her eyes and then down at the ground. "When did you get here?"

"Just a few minutes ago, in time to see your performance with that Basque girl."

"That's really good sport, Gloria. Want to try it with me?"

"No, no, thanks, not with you anyway. I don't want to get kicked and thrown all over the place."

"Hey, did you hear, I bought a new car."

"Really!," she said excitedly.

"Yeah, come on and I'll show it to you."

"Okay, let's go."

Taking Gloria by the arm, Lenny lead her out of the crowd, and when they were away from the lights and among the shadows of the trees, he began to sense the soft warm flesh of her bare arm. The sweet flames of desire began creeping into his blurry consciousness. He let go of her arm and began a half-sober fight to extinguish the blushing sparks within him.

"There's the little jewel," he said when they reached the car.

"Really! Lenny, where did you get it? Why, it's beautiful. Will you take me for a ride in it?" Gloria said turning her big brown eyes from the car to gaze at his tanned face with the long dark hair falling over his forehead.

"Sure, hop in," he said opening the door for her and shutting it with a slam.

He started it up, and they left the park in a loud deep-throated roar. He drove through town and out on a boulevard that lead to the highway that crossed the desert to the southeast. They went out a few miles and then Lenny turned off on a road that would take them back to the city by another route. There was little traffic on this road, and it was dark and winding. Lenny drove at a moderate speed, and they listened to the symphonic low rumble of the motor and the deep chanting of the exhaust pipes.

Lenny had his hand resting on the gear shift knob which sprouted from the floor between them. In the soft roaring silence, she laid her hand on his and moved her fingers into the grooves of his knuckles.

"Gloria, I-"

"Yes," she said softly.

"Nothing, I was just gonna say --."

"Yes."

"Nothing."

He had to slow down for a sharp curve. When they started into the curve, he crammed it into second gear and tromped down on the gas peddle. The tires squealed, and they roared out of the curve onto a straightaway like a bullet. He shifted into 3rd leaving a black puff of smoke and a thunderclap behind them. They picked up speed until the front wheels began to shimmy before Lenny slowed down the panting orange monster.

"It's got guts, doesn't it," he said.

"The car? Yes, it has guts all right. But you don't."

"What do you mean by that," Lenny said, becoming a little angry. No one could say that to him and get away with it without a fight or an apology.

"Nothing," she said.

"What do you mean, nothing?"

"Oh, nothing."

They were coming into the city again into the streetlights and side streets. Nothing more was said, but Lenny glanced over at her once and saw her leaning against the door sad and beautiful. The shadows of the trees and the light of the corner lamps played with her dark thick hair and her tanned softness, and her tantalizing warmth shown through the fingers of light and dark as if through a veil. She wore a yellow flower in her hair. He noticed her blouse blooming and receding with each beat of her deep breathing. She was wearing a pink lipstick which changed into a blue with each flickering shadow. She did not look at him.

When they reached the picnic grounds, there were not any more spaces in the parking area, so Lenny had to drive around on the lawn in back of the lights and people, and among the tall trees and hedges. When he stopped the car, she jumped out and called him "chicken". She had found a bait that he would grab for and threw it at him and ran. He chased and caught her. They scuffled playfully falling to the ground behind a large bush. She was laughing and breathing hard. The top of her blouse had been torn and her white lace bra was visible. Lenny had her arms pinned to the ground, pretending he didn't notice. His blue eyes met her brown ones, and they bubbled together in the champagne of desire. Then, their lips met and he let go of her arms and she entwined them winsomely around his neck.

They lay in an embrace on the cool grass, and she whispered in his ear, "Do you love me?" Lenny did not know what to say. He had never told a girl that he loved her before-not even Karen. He was afraid to say it. She looked hurt when he did not answer and started to get up. Lenny said, "Yes," before he realized the words had come out and so she lay back down.

"Say it," Gloria whispered. She was lovely. Lenny tried to kiss her again. She held him back. "Say it," she said again.

"I love you," Lenny said and then kissed her hard. The sweetness of sin enthralled him. "I must not go further," and he kissed her again. Their hearts were pounding. He quickly pulled away. Lenny was confused, since he never came this close to this kind of sin before. He was slipping on a black sweet ecstatic abyss. He had gone too far. He tried to shake the emotion holding every nerve in its burning soft tight tentacles. She saw his frustration but, he had already bit the bait once, and she set the hook with the same word, "chicken," and the barb stung. "God have mercy," he prayed and kissed her savagely. The lips parted, their tongues met, and she put his hand inside her blouse on her heaving breasts.

She had thrust the shining red apple into his mouth, and he had bitten, and it was juicy and sweet with the spice of sin-sweeter than he had ever imagined it would be.

Chapter Eleven
Agony of Guilt

Lenny had sinned grievously. The delicious apple which was so sweet last night failed to digest in his conscience-ridden self. It nauseated him in the morning. He could think of nothing but his own depravity. He could not eat breakfast. He did not talk to his Mother. Lenny cursed the nuns and priests for telling him that sexual pleasure outside of marriage was wrong. He wished he had never learned what was right and what was wrong. He had known other boys who had made it with girls, and it never seemed to bother them afterwards. They even boasted of it. Boasted of a sin! Boasted of defying God! They had spit on and kicked Jesus when He was down! And they boasted of it!

But those boys did not know it was a sin. They had not been taught it was a sin by priests and nuns, and that they would be damned and suffer hell-fire, if they did not repent. He knew it was a sin. He had spit in the face of God; he had scourged Christ with the whip of iron pieces and smiled when the jagged iron ripped and tore the flesh from His sweaty body. He had pounded the thorns into the head of

Christ. He smiled to see the thick blood run down his forehead and cheeks, and drop off the end of his nose and land on his beard, or run down the contortions of His agonized visage. He had thrown the heavy cross on His beaten shoulders and taunted Him, pushed, and cursed Him. He had beaten Christ when he fell from weariness and pain. He had spit in anger at the woman who wiped the blood, the sweat, and tears off the soiled face of Christ as he stumbled blindly over the rocks under the weight of the heavy cross and His own foul body liquids. He had laughed with glee as he cruelly tore the robes from Christ's body that had adhered to every crusted wound so that the wounds opened again to drip the last drops for the sins of man. He had meticulously selected the rustiest nails and the heaviest hammer and pounded them with fury into the hands and feet of the prostrate Christ who jerked and groaned with pain at each hammer blow. He had cursed the heaviness of the cross, and Christ's body, as he lifted it from the ground and then he laughed sadistically and madly for three hours as the innocent and bleeding Christ hung there- hung there- hung there. Then in a fit of anger at the endurance of Christ, he had taken a spear and thrust it into Christ's side as he cried out to His God and gave up His spirit.

And after he killed Christ so maliciously, he dropped to his knees and cried with his head in his hands. He cried from sorrow and from fear. He had killed Christ, and now it was Christ's turn to punish him. "God have mercy! God have mercy!" he prayed, "for I knew not what I was doing. Christ have mercy on me! Forgive me my sin! Most blessed and pure sweet Virgin Mary pray for me. Forgive me for crucifying your son! Forgive me! Forgive me!"

Lenny had slept late on Monday morning and when he did not speak and did not eat any breakfast, his Mother thought that he might be ill.

"Don't you feel good," she asked him.

"I don't feel worth a damn."

"Let me feel your forehead."

"No! I'm all right. Just leave me alone," he said pushing her hand away.

"Did you get in another fight last night? You got some marks on your face."

"No, no, I didn't get into any fight. Just leave me alone."

"Where are you going now?"

"I don't know," he said leaving the house and letting the screen door slam behind him.

He got in his car and drove to the foothills. He left the black pavement road that was a margin between the city and the foothills on the north and drove over a winding, dusty, and steep road that took him high up over the city and valley to the top of Tablerock. Tablerock was a high mesa that stood impressively over the whole valley, and from the top you could see the city of Boise with its river running through it dividing it in equal halves. While, you could see the green farmlands west of the city and grey desert to the east, far away across the valley, you could barely see the outline of another rugged range of powder-blue mountains whose peaks had proudly punched through the nebulous white haze of the desert and the narrow sheets of clouds.

The road wound around the wide base of the mesa and undulated its way up from the back to the barren flatness of its top. When Lenny reached the top, he drove across the rocky dirt up to the edge overlooking the city. He parked the car and walked along the sharp dark cliffs at the edge while the wind blew ripples in his shirt and pants. The cliffs were from twenty to fifty feet straight down on this side, and ended in a mass of black volcanic boulders and sharp rocks which contrasted sharply against the dull brown of the sloping hill below them.

Sitting down on the edge and letting his feet dangle over it, Lenny sat there with his head bowed and his chin in the palms of his hands, meditating and praying for guidance, strength, and forgiveness. He felt very weary and broken under the burden of his sin while the wind quibbled and played with his hair. His face was tense and fearful when he realized he would have to confess his sin. Lenny thought why did I do it? How I wished I had not done it. He tried to make himself believe that it was all a dream. That he had dreamed what had happened. He had dreams before about loving women-even to the extent that it had caused nocturnal emissions. When this happened and before he even woke up, he would feel regret and contrition because he had sinned. But always when he became fully conscious in the morning, he would realize it had only been a dream, and he felt relief that he had not actually sinned and participated in the risqué happenings of the dream. He'd tell himself, you can't control your dreams, and dreaming isn't a sin. Dreams are natural and even nocturnal emissions are natural. The priests always said that as long as a person was asleep and did not take willful pleasure in the emission, there was no sin.

But sitting on the edge of the rocky cliff and feeling the cool wind coasting down from the mountains on his back, Lenny knew that what had happened last night was no dream. He actually had intercourse with a girl and in doing it, he had sinned grievously. He had never felt this miserable and fearful for his soul at any time in his whole life. Lenny thought what if I should die? "I would certainly go to hell and suffer forever in the undying flames. I would never be able to experience the peace and joy of seeing God in heaven. I would never attain my blissful end." Lenny felt he was the worst sinner that had ever lived, and he began sinking into the despair of the damned souls who writhe and scream in the black torture chasms of hell.

Lenny had thought for a moment of jumping over the cliff and killing himself, ending all his misery. He saw a rock that looked the most jagged and cruel, but it was ten or fifteen feet away from the base of the cliff, and he might not land on it. And, what if it did not kill him and only injure him and break some bones? Then he would lay there and suffer more, perhaps for days before anyone came and found him. It would be just like the rock not to kill him, but only wound him painfully, and then stand over him triumphantly and grinning at the foolishness of another mortal.

Lenny knew from what he had been taught that if he committed suicide that he would certainly go immediately to hell. It would be another great sin, greater than the sin of lust, as no one had any rights over one's own body, because it belongs to God. Lenny had used his own body selfishly for lustful pleasures in defiance of the good and merciful God. Even so, he could not then end his own life-the life God gave to him.

Lenny grabbed his contorted face in his hands and began to sob and utter over and over again, "Oh God! Oh God!," until the wind cooled the warm tears and dried them on his face. His abdomen which had been heaving with the sobbing felt like it was in the grip of a tight iron claw, and it made him feel sick. He thought he would vomit and waited for the foul contents to surge upwards and out of his mouth. But it never happened, and he got up to start walking back to the car and to get out of the wind, which was now wheezing through the dry grass and chasing the dust into swirls and gyrations.

He got into his car and sat there trying to think this thing out. But, his thoughts and images became more of a tangled mass of passion and confusion.

Lenny thought of Gloria, and the forbidden desires began to relive and surge through the morass of remorse that had engulfed him. He tried to fight her naked image, and the memory of that bittersweet moment behind the bushes, and he prayed to the Blessed Virgin to help him. But, he thought she could not hear him while he was in sin. He must go to confession. But, how could he tell the priest the terrible thing he had done? He was terrified with the dread of the moment when he must confess his sin to the priest. He would have to wait until Saturday to go to confession. Today was only Monday. He would have to go through a whole week of this misery. He did not think he could stand to be tortured like this for a whole week. Anything could happen in a week. What if he should see Gloria again during this time? What would he say? What would he do? He must not see her again, or he would certainly sin again, in desire, if nothing else. He did not want to sin anymore. He wanted only to have the peace that comes from being pure of mind and heart.

Trying to decide what to do, Lenny reached for a cigarette, lighting it with trembling hands. He took a big drag and let the smoke settle in his lungs. He resolved to go to confession next Saturday. He would tell the priest everything, and the priest would forgive him, so that he could begin life over again. He would never see Gloria again, and he would never be alone again with any girl, not even Karen, because he knew he could never trust himself again. His character had been dealt a blow, almost a fatal one. He was suffering miserably, but he might yet recover. But the scar would always be there, ugly, tender, sore, and vulnerable. He must forever guard himself against such moral catastrophe. He could never be alone again with a girl.

Now, Lenny would try to pray. He got out of the car, knelt on the dirt, and crossed himself. Bowing his head, he began the Act of Contrition. When he was through, he lifted his face toward the moving white clouds in the sky, and repeated three times, "Christ have mercy!"

Feeling better, Lenny got into his car, and began the drive home. The sun was high in the sky, and it beat down on the little orange car as it wound up, down, and around the hilly brown plateau. Suddenly it swerved off the road and into the dry grass and sagebrush. Lenny had stopped the car. His face was pale and tense. He felt drops of cold sweat trickle from under his arms and down his sides. Lenny thought what if she became pregnant? What will he do then? She couldn't. She mustn't. But, it was possible. Isn't that how babies are made?

At the time, he wished he had a rubber. But, he never had any. He never carried those things. He always despised them and those who carried them in their wallets and boasted about them. He remembered how he used to despise the little dirty-haired seventh graders who used to try and sell them to the ninth graders in the lavatories of North Junior High. He never bought any. Why would he want them? He never intended to have intercourse with a girl. Besides, what if his Mother would have discovered them? Or what if Karen or some of the other girls would have accidentally found them in his wallet? Girls are always wanting to look at the pictures in boys' wallets.

After sitting there for a few minutes, Lenny realized he could do nothing but wait. Lenny thought it was possible Gloria would not become pregnant, and then everything would be all right. But, if she did become pregnant, what would he do? He would have to marry her. Yes, he would marry her. After all he did love her, didn't he? She was beautiful and would make a good wife. But, he did not have any money. How could he support her? Her parents had money, and maybe they could help him find a job. Her parents would help them. He knew that because they would do all they could to make their daughter happy. It might not be so bad after all.

Lenny had been poor all of his life. He had never had many of the nicer things of life, because his parents could not afford them. His Father worked as a laborer after having failed at dry-ranching on their homestead in the foothills and the money he made was barely enough to live on. Now, he could marry into money and live comfortably for the rest of his life. It would not be bad at all. Maybe what had happened would turn out good after all.

But, he could not delude himself. He knew that what happened was not good. Evil was never good and could not be the cause of good. If by telling one small lie, you could save a whole nation from destruction, you still cannot tell the lie because the lie would be evil. You can never do evil hoping that good will come from it. The end never justifies the means. The nuns had told him this, and he had to believe what he was told because he was a Catholic. They were supposed to teach the word of God and the precepts of Christ. It did not seem reasonable to him. Why would it be better not to tell a little lie than to have a whole nation perish? Was it because no lies and no sins can be little? He did not know. Lenny did not understand, but yet he still must believe. He always tried to believe everything that the nuns and priest told him. He was afraid not to. Lenny had to believe or else he would not have faith. If you did not have faith, it meant hell for certain. The most terrible thing that could happen was to lose one's faith. He was frightened of hell. Lenny hated the suffering and the pain in this life, and he tried to avoid it whenever he could. But, the pain of hell was unending and unendurable, yet the lost souls must endure it. There was no escape from hell. The nuns told him that.

Lenny wondered if he was sorry for his sins mostly because they offended God or mostly because he was afraid of going to hell. Sometimes, he did not know. Most of the time, Lenny thought he was sorry because otherwise he would go to hell. This kind of contrition was enough for God to forgive him in confessional, but outside the confessional, and the absolution of a priest, this was not good enough. The nuns taught that it took "perfect contrition" for a person's sins to be forgiven without the absolution of a priest. Was he sorry for what he had done solely because he had offended God? Did he have a firm intention to avoid sin in the future and all the occasions and temptations that might lead him into sin? He did not know. All Lenny knew for certain was that he wanted an end to the warfare going on within him as a result of his sinning by having the wonderful over the top experience of intercourse with Gloria, and to experience once again the peace of a quiet conscience.

Chapter Twelve
Confession

When Saturday finally came, Lenny woke up early, full of anxiety and apprehension because today he would be going to confession. After breakfast, he began to feel a little relief from the strain that he had been under all week. All week long under the stigmata of sin, he had tried to reinforce himself for the moment of revelation to the priest, and with the reinforcing came a layer of hardness bordering on mental torpidity. Confession did not begin until four o'clock, and Lenny decided to work on his car until then. There were a number of things needing to be fixed-the hole in the radiator, a short-circuit in the headlight wires, adjusting the brakes and various other little things that had shaken loose or quit functioning properly.

When four o'clock came, he was still working on the car. He had old clothes on, and they were covered with grease and dirt. His hair was dusty and messed up, and the back of his white T-shirt was black from lying under the car while trying to tighten up the brakes. He still had not found the trouble with his lights, so he decided he would try to fix them before he went to confession. They heard confessions until eight o'clock so he had all evening to go.

By the time he had found the bare wire to the headlights and wrapped friction tape around it, it was time for supper. He washed his hands, but ate supper in his dirty clothes. Lenny was hungry from working all day, but he could not eat much. The hour of shame was drawing near when he would tell the priest everything. Then the full realization of what he had to tell the priest stormed into his consciousness, leaving it a bedlam of disgrace and fear. He stopped eating and stared down at the table.

"Lenny," his Mother said, "Hurry and finish your potatoes, and we'll have dessert. I baked a nice apple pie today."

Lenny did not hear her and kept staring at the table.

"Lenny!" his Mother said again, "Did you hear me? Are you sick? You've been acting funny all week."

"Huh, oh I'm okay, Mom."

"No, you're not. You look pale. You shouldn't have stayed so long in the hot sun fooling with that hot rod."

"I'm okay," he said irritably, pushing back his chair, and getting up from the table.

"Don't you want any pie?"

"No, no, I don't want no pie," he said going into his room. Shutting the door, he sat down on the bed. He felt weak. Holding his head in his hands, Lenny began to perspire. He sat there a few minutes, then looking up at the small crucifix hanging over his bed he pleaded, "God help me! Mary give me strength!"

Lenny kicked off his shoes and slid out of his dirty clothes, leaving them in a pile on the floor by the bed, put on his robe, and went into the bathroom to take a bath. After he was dressed, Lenny walked slowly to his car and made the dreaded drive to the cathedral.

Lenny threw his cigarette away as he descended the steps to the little chapel in the basement of the cathedral. His steel heel plates clicked on the cement, and the heavy door banged shut behind him as he entered among the somber shadows of the chapel. He tip-toed to a pew and knelt down to examine his conscience. He did not need to search back through his memory for vague or forgotten sins this time; he remembered clearly what he had done. He was acutely aware of what he must do.

There were other people in the chapel. Some were kneeling in the pews, and some were standing in line waiting to enter the confessional. Lenny tried to remember when he had gone to confession last. It had been before Easter. He tried to remember some of the venial sins he committed during this time. They were all small ones, and he did not have to mention them in confession if he did not want to, but the big one, the one with Gloria-he had to tell. His hands became wet with sweat, and his head sank down between them. He tried praying to the Blessed Virgin and to his guardian angel. To tell this sin to the priest was the hardest and most difficult thing he had ever had to do. But, he had to do it or live in fear and agony until he did.

More people were coming into the chapel now, and the line to the confessional was getting longer. He had to get it over with as quickly as possible. He summoned all the forces of his will and energy together and got up to stand in line. He stood waiting only a few minutes, but it seemed like hours. He tried to rehearse in his mind how he would tell his sin, deciding he would try to be cool, objective, and mention his lesser sins immediately after the terrible one.

The man before him in line stayed a long time in the confessional, and Lenny thought he must have had some wicked sins too. He wondered how long he would be within the four narrow walls of blackness, with the little window with the cloth over it. In that dark closet, the descriptions of the vilest, most pernicious, abominable and rancid expressions of human depravity and weakness passed into the ears of the priest. The priest, the human instrument of God, had the awful power to wash away the most diabolical and detestable sins from the human soul.

Just as he opened the door to enter the confessional, he glanced at the name of the priest who was hearing confessions on the middle door of the confessional box. It said "Rector". Lenny hesitated with his hand on the door handle- that would be Monsignor O'Toole. He felt faint and sweat began oozing through his forehead. How could he tell the Monsignor? Monsignor O'Toole had known him since grade school, and he would know it was Lenny behind the curtain in the confessional. Monsignor O'Toole was the hardest one to tell sins to, especially sins of impurity, because he would ask questions and give a long discourse of instructions and methods to avoid this particular sin in the future. Sometimes, he gave terrible descriptions of the scourging and crucifixion of Christ to show the effects of our sins on the all-merciful God who died because of them.

But, Lenny had to go in. It was too late to turn back now. Everyone would see him and wonder what was wrong with him. He went in, knelt down, and buried his face in his hands. His fingers slid over his wet forehead and dug into his skin. He could hear Monsignor O'Toole mumbling the prayer of absolution in Latin for the person on the other side. Soon, it would be his turn.

The door on the window slid open, and Lenny could see through the cloth the outline of Monsignor O'Toole's round face and balding head with a few long white hairs combed back over it.

Monsignor uttered the sign of the cross in Latin and crossed himself quickly. His lips trembling, Lenny began, "Bless me Father, for-for I have sinned. My last confession was four months ago."

"I-have-had sexual intercourse with a girl once, and I have had impure thoughts and desires many times. I have used the Lord's name in vain and have missed my daily prayers. I am sorry for these sins and all the sins of my past life especially for—sins of impurity."

"Is there anything else now my son?"

"No, Monsignor."

"How old are you my child?" The priest did not look at Lenny when he asked the question but straight at the rosary in his hands.

"Seventeen."

"And the girl?"

"I don't know, about the same I guess," Lenny said wetting his lips. His mouth was dry and sticky.

"How long have you known the girl?"

"About two years."

"Have you been going together all this time?"

"No, Monsignor. We just happened to be together one night and it-just- happened."

"Were you planning to marry the girl?"

"No-I don't think so."

"Have you ever done this before?"

"No, Monsignor." Lenny wanted to get it over with and get out of there. How long was he going to ask questions?

"Is she a Catholic girl?"

"No, Monsignor."

Monsignor leaned closer to the cloth, and Lenny could hear his deep breathing. "You realize now that this is a very serious sin. You say you've never done it before?"

"No, Monsignor," Lenny said wiping the moisture from his forehead and wetting his lips again.

"Who began this act of sin?"

"I -I Don't know Monsignor. We kissed a couple of times and – and -."

"I See. Now, you're sorry my child and will never do it again?"

"Yes, Monsignor."

"You realize now, my son, the extent that kissing and petting can lead to."

"Yes, Monsignor."

"Sex is a wonderful and beautiful thing when it takes place within the lawful relationship of husband and wife; but outside of marriage, it becomes hideous and depraving. Lust is one of the great evils we have to be on our guard against every day. Your body is the temple of the Holy Ghost and when you sin, you drive God from your soul. You tell God to get out; you tell Him you don't want him anymore-that you have found something else-some thing-to replace Him. God was humble enough to become man and die on the cross a cruel death of ignominy for your sins. The same God gave you existence and whose love of you keeps you in existence. The same God wants you-a mere mortal and sinner-to share with Him one day in the glories and happiness of heaven in company with the saints and angels. We have no right to happiness and Heaven, but the all-good God wants to give them to us because He loves us so much. And you turned away from God, and by your sin, you have struck the chained Christ another cruel blow with the whip of jagged iron."

Lenny tried to check the tears of true sorrow, but they came trickling down his cheeks.

"You must try to drive impure thoughts from your mind. Every time one occurs, say this little prayer, "Mother of purity, pray for me." And then try to occupy your mind with something else that interests you. And above all, my son, you must try to never be alone with any girl again because if you do, you are asking for trouble. It would be like playing with fire, and if you play with fire, you're going to get burned. Do you understand?"

"Yes, Monsignor."

"For your penance, now say two rosaries and make the Stations of the Cross. Now, make an Act of Contrition."

Lenny said the Act of Contrition, and the priest said his absolution. Then Monsignor asked Lenny to pray for him. Lenny said he would, thanked Monsignor, and went to say his penance. It was a long penance, the longest he had ever gotten. But Lenny was glad to do it, and he said every prayer slowly and fervently.

Lenny walked out of the basement chapel of the cathedral and breathed deeply the pure fresh air of the softly falling night. He felt clean and warm inside; his heart was light, his thoughts were buoyant and airy, and he felt his burning conscience grow dull and cool under the healing mist of forgiveness and grace. A great soothing and elevating peace was flowing into his spirit; he felt renewed vigor and strength pour into the gaps and cavities left by the fatigue and decay of his sin.

He was startled by the embellished and adorned world he now saw after rising from the black and ugly pit of remorse he had been in all week. In the West, where the sun was low in the sky, there was still a rosy faint glow squeezing through the blackening lace of the tree branches and the restless slumber of the leaves. Under the roof of the cathedral and between the mortar of large rough and grey stones, a white pigeon lit, fluttered its wings a few times, and then bowed its drowsy head to dream. The silhouettes of the statues of Saints and Apostles stood atop the cathedral, gazing out over the city with their blind eyes. A very old couple, their faces furrowed by the rake of time, shuffled past him slowly and descended the steps to the chapel one at a time clutching and leaning upon the stairway rail. Lenny remembered when he was in grade school and used to play on the steps, and how he could make one running leap from the top, clear the entire stairway and land down at the bottom with an echoing clatter. The old man painfully opened the heavy door and the murmuring sound of the recitation of the rosary swelled through the opening only to be quelled as the door banged shut again.

"Hello, Lenny."

"Oh, hello Father. I didn't see you coming. How have you been?"

"Fine Lenny, and you."

"Oh, I been okay, I guess. Gee, I haven't seen you all summer."

"No, I've been back at Notre Dame for six weeks studying Canon Law. I hope you've been staying in shape this summer. Looks like you've gained a few pounds. How much do you weigh now?"

"I don't know, about a hundred and eighty, I guess. Why?"

"Good. I got a chance to talk to one of the assistant coaches while I was there, and I mentioned you to him, and showed him some of your newspaper clippings and pictures. He was impressed by your records. If you have another good year, you'll have a chance for a football scholarship at Notre Dame."

"No kidding Father! I can't believe it! Why, that would be great, going to Notre Dame! Do you think I have a chance?"

"Sure do, otherwise I wouldn't have gone to the trouble of looking into the possibility. You're the best high school quarterback in the state, and if you play like you did last year, we'll get you into Notre Dame."

"Thank you Father. Thank you very much. I never dreamed I'd get to go to Notre Dame. I thought perhaps I had a chance at Boise J.C. or the University of Idaho, but Notre Dame! Say, what about Angel? Heck, he's a good enough fullback for any team."

"I agree with you, but his grades aren't high enough for Notre Dame anyway. By the way, how are your grades?"

"Okay, about a B average, I guess."

"Good, keep them up too."

"I'll try. I understand we got a lot tougher schedule this year."

"Sure we do, but if we don't win all our games this year with the material we got, I'll quit coaching. Our first three games are the toughest, but if we can win them, we shouldn't have much trouble with the rest."

"Who's our first game with?"

"Mason City."

"Mason City! They've been undefeated the last two years."

"I know and I had to do some talking to get a game with them. Then we play the Nazarenes again-they're always tough-and Donnelly."

"We can take the Nazarenes, but Donnelly- they slaughtered us last year. Them big farm boys are sure tough. I think some of them must have been in high school for eight years."

"Sure, they beat us, but you guys are tough too. Our line lost its guts that's all. I'm going to start practice a week early this year and see if we can't sweat the nicotine out of some of the boys early. By the way, what do you have in your pocket Lenny, a candy bar?"

"Uh, no, where Father?"

"In here," Father O'Connell said as he pulled a pack of cigarettes from Lenny's shirt pocket and looked him in the eye.

"I-I smoke one once in awhile Father," he said squirming a little. "But, I'm going to quit."

"When?"

"Uh, right now, here Father, you keep them. I promise I won't touch another one."

"In that case just so they won't be wasted, and you won't be tempted, I'll take them. Thank you, Lenny. Well, I have to hurry in and relieve Monsignor in the confessional. See you."

"Bye Father, and thanks again."

Lenny turned and ran down to his car which was parked at the curb. He was glad Monsignor had heard his confession and not Father O'Connell. He could never have told Father O'Connell, his football coach, what he had done. The easy and friendly relationship that existed between the two of them would have been broken. Father O'Connell would have recognized Lenny and, even though a priest is supposed to forget all the sins he hears in the confessional, how could he completely forget the recollection of such a vile sin, and how could he ever retain his good opinion and attitude towards him? Lenny thought "Thank God it was Monsignor!" He never really favored Lenny over the other boys like Father O'Connell had, nor did he favor one person over another. He was the shepherd over his whole parish flock, and so he watched and guarded everyone as best he could; but he always remained at a proper distance from any one of them in particular.

Lenny slid behind the wheel of his car, flipped the ignition switch, jammed his foot on the starter, and drove downtown to the Evergreen. He parked his car in the alley because there were no parking spaces in front. Entering the back door, he saw Danny and Angel through the noisy crowd of Levis, suntans, colorful Hawaiian and checkered shirts and white T-shirts. They were both slouched in chairs opposite one of the snooker tables, and each one had a long cue stick propped up between his legs and resting on the floor. Angel was smoking a cigarette. Danny sat there staring at the table. A clump of straight, greasy, cardboard-colored hair hung down over his eyes.

"Hi gents. How is every little thing," Lenny said, walking up to them and sitting in an empty chair next to them.

"Hi, Len," they said.

"How's the game going?"

"Not worth a tinker's damn," Danny said.

"Davis beating you again? Hi Jack."

"Hi Len," Jack said driving in another red ball.

"Hey, guess what. I saw Father O'Connell tonight."

"Yeah, where?" Angel asked.

"Over at the cathedral and--."

"The cathedral-you mean <u>church?</u> What the hell you doing there?" Jack said sarcastically.

"Nothin', I went to confession is all."

"Confession? What's the occasion?"

"Nothing, I felt like going. I hadn't been for a long time."

"Oh, did the priest forgive all your-what do you call 'em-sins, and tell you to be a good boy and not to beat your meat anymore," Jack laughed mockingly.

Lenny turned red and felt like telling Jack to go to hell, but he did not say anything. He never did like Jack Davis very much. Jack was too much of a wise guy and a bully. He remembered the night of the junior party when Jack threw sand in a kid's eyes, and then beat him up for no reason at all except to have a little sport and show everyone what a tough guy he was. Lenny wondered if Jack would fight him if he told him to "eat shit" and asked him to come out in the alley if he wanted to make something of it. Jack never fought anyone his own size on fair terms, and Lenny was as big and strong as Jack was. Seeing that he had pissed Lenny off, Jack stopped smiling and began to sight in his cue for another shot.

Lenny turned to Danny, and said, "Anyway, Father says we're going to start practice a week early and--."

"A week early, how come?"

"To sweat the nicotine and beer outa you guys, that's how come."

"Us. Look who's talking," Danny said.

"I'm quittin' and going into training right now."

"I don't see no hurry about it. Gimme a cigarette Basco."

"Creepy, you're the worst leech there is. Well, whadya know, Davis missed one. Your shot, Creep."

"Anyway, ya know who we play first?" Lenny continued. "Mason City."

"No caca! They're the state champs. Hey Creep, didya hear that? We play Mason City the first game."

"No mung! Curve ball! Curve you chicken monger!" The ball didn't quite go in the pocket.

"Pee and moan Creepy," Angel said, getting up and taking aim on a red ball in the side pocket.

"I can't wait to start playing again. I feel like we could trounce Mason City," Danny said coming back over and sitting down.

"Me too. But they're going to be tough. Not only that, but the next two games are with the Nazarenes and Donnelly."

"We'll club the Nazarenes."

"Remember, we were going to club them last year, and they beat us 20 to 14."

"Yeah, but every time we go over there we have to play fourteen men. I wonder what they pay their damned officials. I'd like to clobber the one who called clipping on me when I dumped that guy that was chasing you when you went eighty yards on the kick-off for a touchdown. This year we'll play them on our field."

"Yeah, the bastards, they called it back," Lenny said. He thought about telling them about the possible scholarship to Notre Dame, but decided not to say anything about it yet.

"By the way, I saw Pat today," Angel said coming back to his seat.

"Is that right?" Lenny said, "Where'd you see him?"

"In the Cave. He got fired for gettin' drunk and not showing up for work."

"No crap. You mighta known he'd screw it up. Surprises me he lasted this long. Wonder if he's home now?"

"Call him up and see. What you gonna do tonight Len? Teddy Bear said to come on out to his pad tonight and listen to some new records and drink a little beer. Gloria said to be sure and ask you to come too. Hey, what is it with you and Gloria anyway?"

"Oh, you know how it is Basco. All the women go for me. It must be my good looks 'cause I sure ain't rich. Yeah, my good looks and my charming personality."

"Cacapeliosa," Angel said, swearing in Basque.

At the mention of Gloria's name, Lenny's mind began to wander back to the night of the Basque picnic. Then he remembered the pain and fear that possessed him after that until his sin had been purged by sorrow and repentance in the confessional. But, the image of her tanned body lying on the grass was still fresh, and he could still recall the redolence of her black hair and the softness of her breasts and firmness of her nipples. These things were hard to erase from his memory. His sense of purity and cleanliness began acquiring a few smudges from the grime and sweat of renewed desire. But his will had been strengthened by his resolution in confession, and he wiped away the image and desire with a short prayer to the Blessed Virgin, the Mother of purity.

The game was over, and Davis had won. Angel put his cue stick in the rack on the wall and sat down next to Lenny.

"Whatdyasay Len. Want to go with us out to Ted's? I got the pickup again."

"Naw, I don't think so Basco. I think I'll go see if I can find Pat."

"Okay, What should I tell Gloria if she asks about you?"

"I don't know. Tell her I couldn't come or something. And don't drink too much beer, or you'll be in hell of a shape for football."

"Yeah, I'm going to start training and quit drinkin' and smokin'- after tonight."

"Okay, remember, after tonight. You too,Danny."

"Me, I'm in great shape. I feel I could whip my weight in wildcats."

"Yeah. You're in great shape, all right. I bet you couldn't run around the block without crappin' out."

"Now, Len—"

"C'mon, great mighty athlete, we're late now," Angel said grabbing Danny by the arm.

"Ouch, take it easy Basco."

"Look at the big strong tough Creepy, ha, ha," Lenny laughed.

"Another word outa you, and I'll knock a turd out of you as long as a pump-handle."

"Please! Please! Creepy, don't do that. I'm sorry. I won't say nothing no more," Lenny said feigning fear.

"All right, we'll see you Len. Just don't push me that's all."

"See ya large Creepy, see ya Basco."

Chapter Thirteen
Search for the Ultimate

Lenny walked through the pool room annex and sat down at the fountain and ordered a vanilla coke. After drinking the coke and crunching the ice between his teeth, he hurried out through the back door and jumped into his car. He roared through the alley in low gear and then let up on the gas and listened to the dual straight pipes snap and crackle. Then he turned out into the street and headed for Patrick's apartment to see if he was home.

At the door to the apartment house, Lenny met Sherry who was leaving.

"Hi Sherry, you're looking lovely tonight. Is Pat home?"

"Hello Lenny, thank you. Yes, the big clod is home," she said and hurried down the steps to a new white Buick convertible waiting in the parking lot.

Mrs. Shea opened the door when Lenny knocked.

"Good evening Mrs. Shea. Is Pat home?"

"Oh, hello Lenny. Yes, he's here. Come in."

Lenny walked in and immediately saw that the telephone was ripped from the wall, and was laying on the living room floor upside down with the receiver a few feet away and underneath a chair. Lenny stared at the telephone and then up at Patrick who was walking toward him in his stocking feet. His face was red and tense.

"Hi Pat, I heard you were in town so I thought I'd stop in."

"Good to see you, Len," Patrick said, shaking his hand and forcing a smile.

"It's good to see you, too. What's new?"

"Nothing much. Same old ratty world, and I am no longer employed."

"That's what I heard," Lenny said glancing at Mrs. Shea. Her face looked very tired, and she was almost in tears.

"Please excuse me," she said in a broken voice, "I'm exhausted, have a headache, and think I'll go to bed."

When she had left the room, Lenny said in a low voice, "What gives around here. Did you have a fight?"

"Yes, but that's nothing unusual in this house. Every time I'm home, there's a fight."

"What happened this time?"

"If that sister of mine would keep her mouth shut and listen to me once in awhile, everything would be all right. I was very nice and spoke softly and tried to make her aware of the risks involved in going out with those damned rich virgin gobblers and tea and crumpet wenches. Then, she had to get smart."

"I hope you didn't actually hit her with the phone."

Patrick looked down at the telephone scattered across the floor and at the hole in the plaster where it originally was and started to laugh.

"Now what made me do a thing like that?"

"Looks like you've literally begun throwing stones, whereas before they've only been verbal."

"Somebody has to stop her before it's too late. My illustrious parents don't seem to give a damn."

"Your father is home?"

"Physically. He's in the house, but he may as well not be. He's passed out in the bedroom, drunk."

Lenny didn't say anything. He just stood there looking down at the floor and the telephone, slowly shaking his head.

"Want a beer?"

"No, I don't think so. I'm going to start training for football."

"Are you sure? I'm going to have one."

"Oh, okay. One won't hurt, I guess."

"Probably do you good. Beer has lots of calories, you know."

Lenny sat down on the couch still gazing at the telephone. He thought, poor Patrick becomes insane when he goes into a rage. It will be a wonder if he doesn't kill someone someday. He heard Patrick opening the beer cans and humming a little tune in the kitchen. It took some strength to rip a telephone clear out of the plaster in the wall but, this mild and frail little man with the mind of a genius, humming in the kitchen, did it in a moment of rage. Lenny was thinking-did he throw the telephone at Sherry or at the thought of what might happen to her in the company of the "rich virgin gobblers"?

"Pardon me for disturbing your meditation Len, but here is your brew."

"Oh, thanks, Pat," Lenny said, taking a long drink of the cold beer. "How long you been in town?"

"I got in last night. I got a ride out of Wallace where we were staying in a hotel."

"Bring you clear to Boise?"

"Yes."

"What's the story about you getting fired? Basco told me you got drunk and didn't go to work. How come you did that?"

"Why did I do that?" Patrick said, setting his can of beer on the coffee table and lighting up a long Pall Mall cigarette and offering one to Lenny who declined it. "I felt like it. I felt like getting drunk and I did. And I'm damned glad that I did."

"I assumed you felt like getting drunk, but how come you felt like it?"

"You really want to know why?"

"Sure."

"Okay, I'll tell you," Patrick said, getting up and starting to pace the floor in his usual fashion. "If I wouldn't have gotten drunk, I would have gone with the other guys on the crew and paid a visit to the prostitute in the room next to ours."

"No mung," Lenny said as his right knee began springing up and down.

“No mung. These two other guys on the crew and me were sitting in our room playing cards when this girl knocks on the door to see if we would be interested in purchasing her body for five bucks each. Both these guys go to the university, and the one that answered the door-it was really humorous- he didn’t know what to say. He just stood there stuttering and mumbling incoherently until she said she would be in the next room waiting and left. Well, after the moment of shock, we all had a big laugh until they got to thinking it over and decided they really would go and buy her body for awhile. “Hell, it is only five dollars, and she was fairly good looking, what I saw of her in the doorway,” one of the guys said.

“Jees! Why would they do a thing like that?” Larry asked.

Patrick stopped pacing and glared at Lenny and shouted, “Why!” Don’t you have a candle burning between your thighs just aching to be quenched by the horny milk!”

“What do you mean?”

“Read Dylan Thomas sometime.”

“I tried once. He’s harder to understand than you are.”

“All right,” he said gently, “if you want me to draw you a picture, I will. Doesn’t your penis start flexing when you are sitting alone in a car on a dark night and holding Karen in your arms or Gloria for that matter?”

"I—I see what you mean," Lenny said fumbling in his empty shirt pocket for a cigarette. Patrick walked over and gave him one, lighting it with his silver lighter.

"Don't you think I didn't want to go with them? Don't you think I don't have a burning candle too? I wanted to go-she was young and looked like she had a lovely body. But, I didn't go-I got drunk instead and stayed drunk all the next day, and I got fired. And I'm glad that I did what I did."

"Son of a bitch," Lenny said and his knee was shaking again. He was wondering if he should tell Patrick about his affair with Gloria. If he could tell anyone, it would be Patrick. He was his best friend, and he thought they understood each other pretty well. True and lasting friendship is welded together by the bond of understanding, and without understanding, friendship is shallow and frail and prey to circumstance or physical distance. But, the friendship based on understanding, which is the main thing that breeds love, is durable and transcends the wastelands of time and space.

But, Lenny decided not to tell even Patrick. He felt a need to tell someone who would understand, other than the priest, but he was a little afraid. He did not know how Patrick would react, and he didn't want to do or say anything that might cause Patrick to think less of him. Especially at this time, since Patrick also had a close call with sin.

"She couldn't have been more than eighteen, and a prostitute!" Patrick mumbled finishing his beer and sitting down on the couch. Neither of them said anything more for a few minutes.

Then Lenny said, "What else you been doing in your travels besides painting white lines and dodging prostitutes?"

"Not much. I've been in a state of mental menopause ever since I started working. I'm rather glad I was canned. Now I'll have a chance to do something."

"Like what?"

"There are some things I have to find out for myself before I really go bughouse."

"Oh, and what are they?"

Patrick ground out the butt of his cigarette and lit another one saying, "Whether there is truly a God, and if there is, what is He like; whether there is a life after death in the form of reward or punishment for the rightness or wrongness of human actions."

"You mean you doubt there is a God and heaven or hell. Why Pat, you've been taught that there are ever since grade school..."

"Sure," he said, "I've been taught a lot of things, and later I find out that all the things I've been taught aren't true. Just because..." and he got up and started to pace the floor again, "I've been told there is a God; does that mean there is?. I quit believing everything anybody tells me, and I'm going to find out for myself. No one has ever proved to me that there is a God, whereas, by God, I've become aware of a lot of evidence in the world that seems to argue that there is no benevolent God that cares about you or me or anyone else. I know one thing. The God they illustrate in grade school Catechism as the wise looking wrinkled old man with the white beard sitting on a big throne on top of the universe-I know that God is a myth and a farce."

"Where do you think you'll find proof of a different God? I'd like to see some proof myself-though don't get me wrong, I still believe there is."

"Maybe I shouldn't talk about it. I don't want to be a danger to your faith," and his voice was filled with intense emotion as he said, "because the most terrible and fatal thing that can happen to a person is the loss of his faith! No one can understand the misery that follows unless he experiences it himself."

"That's okay, Pat. I can see how it would be really tough to face the world without any-any- uh, sustaining faith. And, I'm not afraid that an idiot like you could weaken mine."

"I'm jealous of you, Lenny, and anyone else who still has a deep faith in God. My faith has been shattered, and I have nothing left to hang on to. And you don't know the feeling of helplessness and anguish that has followed. I can't stand it any longer. I have to search now-for something-I have to find something to believe in. I want to believe in God and Christianity, but I cannot believe in them any longer. But, I'm going to look for answers until I'm certain one way or the other."

"Where are you going to look?"

"I'm going to start with those," he said pointing to a stack of thick books on his desk.

"What are they?"

"Books on philosophy- Schopenhauer, Acquinas, Nietzche, Hume, Saint Augustine, Durant, Plato, and so on."

Lenny almost asked what philosophy was, but he didn't want to show his ignorance so instead he asked, "What if you don't find any proof and end up an-what do they call someone who doesn't believe in God?"

"An atheist."

"Yeah, that's it."

"If I become thoroughly convinced there is no God, then I shall commit suicide."

"Commit suicide!"

"Yes, certainly. That would be the logical thing to do. In this world, there is no lasting joy, nor happiness, nor peace, and the only thing that could sustain me through this mortal valley of tears would be the hope for happiness in a hereafter. If there is no God and no life after death, then I see no use in living because to live is to suffer. And, I'm damned tired of suffering."

"But Pat, there is a God, and there is a life after death. The nuns and priests have told us that, and they should know."

"I know what they've told us," he said impatiently, "but, show me where God is. Have you ever seen God or met someone who has come back from the dead to tell you about what's beyond? Tell me where I can find this good and beautiful God, and if I have to crawl around the world on my hands and knees to reach him, I will. If there is a God, show me where He is, and I will adore, I will serve humbly, and I will beg Him to forgive me-to have mercy on me for all that I have done wrong! And, all that the human race has done wrong!"

Lenny did not say anything. He did not know where God was, and he could not prove His existence or prove that man has an afterlife. He had never questioned these things and had always believed them because the nuns had told him, and he always thought the nuns were right. They wouldn't lie. He had never met anyone before who doubted these things, and he was becoming quite troubled about the whole matter.

Lenny couldn't believe his best friend was having these doubts-the person whom he had admired so much for his intelligence and his wide learning, for his ability to speak his thoughts so well, for his grace and kindness, and for his courage to act according to his beliefs. Patrick could explain and defend certain points about religion better than anyone else in school, and he used to be an altar boy and would frequently attend mass, even on weekdays. He never used to do anything wrong or get into trouble; he never used to misbehave in school or get into fights, he never used to swear, and he had received many awards and prizes for getting high grades. This same person was now doubting the existence of God and the validity of Christianity.

In grade school, when the rest of the fellows would suggest anything wrong or mischievous like de-pantsing the younger boys or throwing snowballs at cars or stealing marbles, he would never participate in these activities.

Lenny remembered the time back in the fifth grade when a group of the older fellows decided to write dirty words and pictures on the walls of the boy's lavatory. Patrick was with them, and they all agreed to write something except Patrick, who said he would not, because it was wrong. They all laughed at first, but then they became angry because he would not do it. They grabbed him and tried to force him by twisting his arm until you could see the pain run through him. He did not try to resist but stood there and silently refused. They jerked and twisted his arm behind his back until he doubled over, his face contorted and writhing. He still refused in spite of the pain, not crying or trying to fight back. Afraid of breaking his arm, the one twisting it let go, and grabbing both arms, held him, while the others hit him as hard as they could in the stomach. At each blow, Patrick just groaned a little louder. The perspiration was seeping through his forehead, and he was becoming white.

Then the boys asked him again if he would write on the wall. His chin resting on his breastbone, he never raised his head, just moved it back and forth. The older fellows were becoming very angry at his obstinacy. It started out merely as a joke, and they thought Patrick would surely give in after a little good-natured physical punishment. But, when he would not submit, even after the beating that they gave him, their pride was hurt. They were all seventh and eighth graders, and here this little pantywaist in the fifth grade was openly defying them and flaunting their commands. This was a matter of principle. They either had to make Patrick obey or lose all the respect that they demanded from the younger boys. They were the kings of the school, and their subjects were all in the lower grades. To refuse was rebellion.

One of them then stepped up to Patrick, and called him a bastard and slapped him hard across the face. A red welt began forming where he hit Patrick and a tear dropped out of the corner of his eye. Lenny was standing in a corner watching all this. He was smaller than any of the bullies, but he could not stand it any longer. Anger and hate had been building up inside him during all this time like a great black mass of thunderclouds that roll in unnoticed from the clear horizon, and it now possessed and blinded him. When the big fellow slapped Patrick, the storm inside him roared, rupturing his usual placidness. He lunged forward and struck the assailant knocking him against the wall. Lenny then leaped around and grabbed the one who was holding Patrick by the throat, and threw him back into the wall urinal where he cracked his head. The rest of them, stunned for a moment by his attack, now closed in on him. Lenny swung and kicked like a wild man, and then ducked and broke through their closing gap. One of them grabbed Lenny by the arm, but Lenny pivoted around and smashed him in the face. The fellow yelled and let go, as blood began streaming from his shattered nose.

The noise brought the Principal of the school, a big middle-aged nun, right into the boy's lavatory. She grabbed the rest of the big fellows by the hair, shaking them and demanding them to stop fighting. Then two other nuns came in, and they were so shocked and scared, they could not do anything but stand there and ask what was happening.

All the boys were all sent to Monsignor O' Toole, who demanded to know the cause of all the disorder. But no one would tell who started the fight or why. They all ended up staying after school for an hour each day for a whole month.

This same Patrick Shea, who had been so adamant in his belief and practice of his religion, had become notorious for getting drunk, wrecking cars, defying lawful authority, missing school, and arguing with the nuns. This happened all within the last year. Now, he was questioning the fundamental tenets of his Christian religion.

While Lenny was thinking about these things, Patrick was still pacing the floor.

“Hey, Pat,” Lenny said, desiring to bring their relationship back into more pleasant circumstances, “you've never seen my car yet, have you? Put on some shoes, and we'll take a run downtown. It's only around eleven o'clock.”

“Sounds great. I want to see this iron beast of yours.”

They drove downtown to Art's drive-in where they had a soda and talked with some of their friends for awhile. Then,

Lenny drove Patrick home and went home himself. When Patrick got upstairs, he threw his shoes off, switched the desk light on and sat down to begin his search for the Ultimate.

At two-thirty in the morning, he was well into a volume of Schopenhauer, and it was at this time that Sherry came in quietly. Patrick did not say anything, but he watched her move across the floor with his eyes blazing. She went over and picked up the pieces of the phone still lying on the floor and said, “You’re not only a wild man, you’re a sloppy housekeeper too.”

Patrick did not answer, but just stared at her. She put the phone on the coffee table and walked over to the closet to hang up her jacket.

“What’s the matter, brother dear, aren’t you going to ask me where I went, what I did, and whether I had a nice time or not?”

He still did not say anything so she kept on talking, “We went to a show downtown-not the passion-pit, as you call the drive ins-and then we went to Ted Ferrel’s pad. A couple of your crude friends from Holy Cross were there- Danny Pankowski and Angel Andarzo. I also met Jack Davis for the first time. I had heard so much about him, and he didn’t seem so bad like the stories you hear. He was surprised to find out that Patrick Shea’s sister was such a “cute chick”.

Patrick spoke for the first time. "It would be extremely difficult to find a halo over his head, my dear. I would not deem it an honor to have met him since he is a bum of the lowest order. And, what it was you may have heard about-if it was bad or vulgar or obscene-was probably true."

"I don't believe it, and you'd better not start standing in the pulpit and preaching to me again. I am old enough to know what I'm doing."

"Yes, child, and how long ago was it that you quit suffering from enuresis?"

"Oh! You Beast! You shut up about that, do you hear, or I'm going right in and tell Mother. You-why you're still just a slobbering little crumgobbler, a squealing little rugrunner, who thinks he knows everything, and what's more, you're mad, too! A madman who goes around raving all the time-like the world is coming to an end or something. You don't see any adults doing that, do you?"

"Listen," Patrick said, getting up and grabbing his sister by the arm, "Listen to me," he tried to speak, but his lips moved, and no sound came out. For the first time in his life, he could not find the proper words to express himself. Finally, he blurted out with quivering emotion, "Davis and those other guys you've been going out with, they're the kind that goes around smelling girls' bicycle seats on hot days. They're virgin gobblers. They're bastards. Dirty Bastards!"

Sherry tried to slap him, but he caught her hand, and said, “Dammit Sherry, they are, they’re like that. Can’t you see, they’re no good for you. Please, I’m only doing this for your sake. Stop it before you get into trouble.” His face was twisted in passionate exhortation.

“If you‘re through blabbering, then let go of me,” she said. She turned and went into her bedroom. Patrick went back to his desk and laid his head in his hands and found himself praying to a God that he was not sure existed.

Chapter Fourteen
Hot Summer Ends

The rest of August was warm and still- the Dog Days of summer. The hot days were becoming shorter, and the nights were starting to cool. The raging young hormones of this hot summer began to subside with the cooler nights of the high desert. Or, were they just getting diverted from the adolescent sexuality to the intensity of high school football- at least for the boys. But, it was the summer. This particular Hot Summer in the High Desert was a special summer to remember.

By the beginning of September the changes in the weather seemed odd and a little weird. Football practice had started, but the beginning of football and school wasn't the same as in previous years. It is hard to explain, but entering the Senior year of high school was strangely different from the years before. Was it because it was the last year to be young and carefree, before having to worry about becoming an adult, with all of the problems associated with that?

The Senior year for Lenny and his friends was rather inconspicuous, nebulous and vague. You went to school, studied, played sports, and dated. You couldn't wait 'til high school was over, so you could get on with your life.

Epilogue

PATRICK

The nuns decided Patrick should not be allowed to return to Holy Cross. Patrick's Father had good connections with the Jesuits at Gonzaga University in Spokane, Washington. Patrick hitch-hiked to Spokane and met with the Jesuits, who agreed to have Patrick take a number of college entrance exams. He easily passed them all, and was admitted as a Freshman, even though he still had not graduated from High School.

Patrick settled down in college and thrived on the high intellectual environment surrounding Jesuit universities. Whether or not he came to believe in Christianity, or a benevolent God, no one knows. But, he graduated from Gonzaga, and married a pretty girl that he had met at Holy Cross High School years before. They had three children-all girls.

If there were predominant features about Patrick, it was that he was enigmatic, unpredictable, and unconventional. After college, he went to work as a social worker for the State of Washington, and was assigned to work at a large Indian reservation in the North Central part of the State, where he spent many years helping the Indians and doing his best to deal with the alcoholism and other problems on the reservation. He became close to Nature, and learned how to fish, hunt, and explore the wilderness of Central Washington. He always had a 4-wheel drive pickup with a rifle, a fishing pole, a Bowie knife, and a six shooter in it. The Real West, far away from the big cities, can do strange things to people. Or, maybe the religion of the American Indians appealed to him more than Catholic Christianity. The concepts surrounding the beliefs of the Native Americans may have brought him some peace, as the Native Americans had a strong belief in a benevolent Creator and a Spirit World of some sort where you went after life on earth. Their concept of the afterlife was not very defined, and it did not include a place equivalent to Hell and eternal damnation. They couldn't conceive of something like Satan and sin, as being part of creation.

In the old days, before the reservations and the forced education of the White Man's ways, the Native Americans were a strange combination of environmental concerns and a benevolent society. But, there was also a strong and fierce Warrior element. They knew how to live with and nourish nature, how to build families and strong communities, but they were also quite ready and willing to defend and fight for their beliefs and the territories that they believed their Creator had given to the various tribes.

Patrick related to the American West, and the Native American, and Mountain Man cultures. He found the best way for him to experience God was by hiking in the mountains, sitting by a river running over rocks in the forest, or laying on his back at night in a sleeping bag and gazing at the stars on a clear night.

After about 20 years of marriage, he and his wife divorced. Patrick died a few years later of mysterious circumstances. He was, in many ways, a living and brilliant enigma, and it was fitting that his passing also fell into this pattern.

SHERRY

Patrick's beautiful sister, Sherry, even though she dated many of the more rogue boys, actually remained a virgin, went away to college, returned to Boise, and married a successful business man. They had a few children, and were a typical family living among the newly wealthy and handsome younger generation who ended up populating the Boise Valley.

DANNY

Danny went to Boise Junior College for a couple years, and studied accounting. He married his girlfriend from high school. They had three children and lived as a typical family that was climbing up the ladder. He started out as a car salesman, and ended up buying the dealership. He sold it for a big profit and then owned and sold many different businesses over the years, including farms growing the famous Idaho potatoes.

Danny raised his family Catholic. His children were all well educated, and they became successful citizens in and around Boise.

FRED

Fred didn't go to college. After High School he started right in to help his Father run the family business, which was a neighborhood grocery store his Father started in the middle of the Depression. Fred married his High School girlfriend, and they had three children. He eventually took the business over and expanded it, but, in the meantime, he would buy real estate from time to time-rental homes, apartments, and commercial buildings. He was always low key in business, and ended up a very wealthy property owner. No one knew 'til many years later that his parents helped him buy his first rental duplex while he was still in High School.

ANGEL

Angel had a good Senior year on the Holy Cross football team. He later went to Boise Junior College and tried out for the team. He made the team, didn't study much, but was one of their first string running backs for two years. This was during the time Boise Junior College was playing top Junior Colleges all across the country. And, they were in the middle of the longest winning streak in college history. They won 60 games in a row over seven seasons. This was the beginning of the Boise State football legacy, which continues to this day. Even though Angel was a fast, tough, and big Basque, and enjoyed playing football for the Broncos, it wasn't so much fun later in life after a number of knee and shoulder surgeries made necessary because of the injuries from this brutal sport. Angel also married his High School sweetheart. They had a typical family. He became a successful business man in Boise, a prominent Alumnae, and important member of the Basque community. He also raised his family Catholic.

GLORIA AND JACK DAVIS

After the passionate night in the city park while the Basque picnic was going on, Lenny and Gloria did not see much of each other anymore. Lenny stayed closer to his friends at Holy Cross, and Gloria did the same at Boise High. Gloria and Jack started going out together and, after High School, in the summer of 1953, Gloria became pregnant. They got married, and both went off to college out-of-state. In the fifties it was not unusual for young married couples to have children while going to college. Before they graduated from college, however, they got divorced. Jack came back to Boise and married a socialite, and ended up being a wealthy politician.

Gloria ended up marrying the son of a successful potato and onion farmer whom she met in college. They moved to a big farm in Southeastern Idaho. The husband took over the operation of the farm, and they had three children. They lived happily ever after, in the starkly beautiful Idaho farming country.

LENNY AND KAREN

For Lenny, the end of the Hot Summer of 1952 was like the last of a marvelous journey-nostalgic, sad, exciting, and sobering. But, there was football to play! And, Lenny was looking forward to a good season, and the prospect of getting a scholarship to a big university-maybe even Notre Dame!

The season started well. Holy Cross won its first three games including the one against Mason City, and Lenny's passing and running were highlighted in every write-up in the Idaho Statesman newspaper. Between running and passing, Lenny counted for two or three touchdowns a game, and Angel usually added a couple of his own, often dragging two or three tacklers with him over the goal line.

Then, in the fourth game against the big tough farmers and ranchers around Bruneau, on a pass option play, Lenny decided to keep the ball and run around the end. He was tackled around the ankles, and the twisting involved caused the left ankle to have a serious break. This ended the football season for Lenny, along with any chance of a college scholarship. It was a bad break, and it never healed well enough for Lenny to even play his Senior year on the basketball team, where he played a forward and had been one of the leading scorers on the team.

The rest of his Senior year was a blur. Lenny never got over the disappointment and disillusion that his athletic career had come to an end. He needed to get over it and move on, but it was really hard to do. Going to school, studying, an occasional party or date with Karen was all that was left. Even shooting pool at the Evergreen became a more or less mechanical and boring event. His pool shooting skills suffered as well, and he started to lose more than he won. Lenny's close friendship with Patrick lessened with him away at college in Spokane. They rarely saw each other from then on, and when they did, it wasn't the same. Under the influence of the Jesuits and the opportunity to pursue intellectual activities, Patrick grew up fast and straightened out his life.

Finally, graduation and preparing for college became uppermost. A summer job in construction, building houses, kept him out of trouble, and on the weekends there were dates with Karen. Their attraction for each other was becoming increasingly intense, but they both made sure that they would never end up going all the way, like it had with Gloria.

Lenny ended up going to Seattle and enrolled at Seattle University. He wanted to go to a Catholic college, just like Patrick did. And, the Jesuits at Seattle University at that time arranged their classes to accommodate students who were working their way through school, like Lenny had to do.

Karen stayed in Boise, working at the telephone company, and waited for him. After two years in college, Lenny and Karen got married, and they got a small apartment near the campus. She worked in a bank and helped him get through college. By the time he graduated, they had one child and another on the way.

Lenny and Karen lived mostly at the poverty level, while Lenny kept going to school until he got his Master's degree in English Literature from University of Washington. While working towards his Masters, he taught Freshmen English at Seattle University. Then, Lenny taught at a local junior college and continued studying at the University of

Washington where he eventually got a Ph. D and was hired by Boise State University as an English Professor.

Lenny and Karen had four children, two girls and two boys. They kept the Faith and raised their children as good members of the Church. After Vatican II, Karen joined the Charismatic movement where she found fulfillment and purpose. Lenny concentrated on finding effective ways to teach the truths and values that fill up great Literature, and how best to raise and care for his family.

If there is a lesson in this tale of the Summer of 1952, it is this. In spite of how one lived, and the crazy things everyone did at the height of hormonal activity while teenagers, most everyone manages to live through it OK, and ends up being rather normal good citizens through the Grace of God!

Made in the USA
San Bernardino, CA
28 January 2015